HANNAH'S HERO

Denise Richards

A KISMET® Romance

METEOR PUBLISHING CORPORATION
Bensalem, Pennsylvania

To Vanessa, thanks for refusing to let me accept less than my best, always answering the phone, and showing me that true friendship does exist in this world.

DENISE RICHARDS

Denise can't remember a time when books weren't an important part of her life. They've helped her escape from reality when dirty dishes and diapers threatened her sanity and even taught her how to drive a standard. As a romance writer and president of her local Romance Writers of America chapter, Denise is convinced that reading is our best hope for the future. Denise lives in Texas with her husband, Rick, and their two sons.

Other books by Denise Richards:

No. 44 *DEADLY COINCIDENCE*
No. 119 *A FAMILY AFFAIR*

PROLOGUE

"Sanchez has made a threat." The tall blond man was more suited to the cover of *GQ* magazine than a dingy diner on a forgotten stretch of highway in south Texas. The waitress refilled his coffee cup, hesitating slightly in case either man should want more than was offered on the menu. No luck.

"The folks?" Only a brief tensing of carefully etched jaw muscles betrayed Kane's concern. He looked much more at home in this washed-out border town. Long dark hair heavily flecked with gray hung on his shoulders and his skin was the shade of finely tanned leather. A thick mustache hid straight teeth and black contacts camouflaged the blue of his eyes but not their intelligence. Kane McCord was an expert at blending into his surroundings. In his line of work, he had to be.

"No. He's promised Hannah won't live to testify." Austin Lee Hardaway watched the man across from him for a reaction. "Our sources say he's afraid his honor will suffer if he doesn't exact some sort of revenge."

"Revenge, hell!" Kane's long fingers curled around the chipped coffee cup. "Wasn't killing my brother enough? What more does the bastard want?"

"Calm down, old man." A.L.'s blue eyes slid around the cafe to see if any of the diners had noticed Kane's outburst. "Hannah's testimony can send him down. She's the only eyewitness. If she's out of the way . . ." He shrugged his shoulders, not needing to finish the statement.

Kane drained the grimy remnants from the bottom of his cup and fished around in the pocket of his worn jeans for change. "Let's get out of here."

Loco, Texas, was aptly named. A man would have to be crazy to live here. Only three miles from the Mexican border, it was merely a refueling station for travelers. Those heading north hoping for jobs, those heading south after the dream fell flat.

And then there were the travelers Kane dealt with. Those needing a quiet place to exchange their goods. Kane had been with the Drug Enforcement Agency for thirteen years and for the last ten he had been living and working in places like Loco, putting people like Roberto Sanchez out of business.

"When is the trial?" Kane asked as he led A.L. off the main street toward the small room he rented over Lupe's Garage.

"In three weeks. He'll have to make a move soon." A.L. kept his voice low and his eyes open as the two men started up the rickety steps leading to the apartment. "This doesn't have anything to do with our operation down here and it'll be my job if Hooper finds out I told you."

"I'm pulling out." Kane thrust the door open before him with his right hand as both men instinctively took defensive positions on either side of the doorframe before entering the dilapidated building. "Fix it with Hooper."

"No way." The blond settled onto the one chair in the room not covered with newspapers and soiled clothes. "The department will never okay it. You're too involved."

"The hell with them." Kane hurriedly stuffed a few clothes into a drab olive-green duffle bag. "I've given up everything for the damned department. They owe me." Kane's eyes sent a clear message even in the dim light filtering through the grime-covered windows. "Hooper doesn't have to know everything."

"Let us handle this." A.L. knew it wouldn't do any good; he understood his friend's rage.

"Right, the way you handled the protection on Seth." Kane rounded on the one man he could honestly call a friend. "In case you've forgotten, my brother's been rotting in a grave for the past eighteen months. I'll take care of his wife."

"You do whatever you have to. I'll clear it with Hooper." A.L. followed Kane out of the room, not bothering to close the door behind them. Kane McCord didn't own anything that couldn't be left behind and he wouldn't be coming back.

ONE

Hannah McCord pulled the brush through her honey-brown hair one more time before tying it back into her usual ponytail. She knew she should cut it, thirty-one was too old to have hair clear down to your waist, but something always stopped her. Sometimes her own vanity, sometimes the memory of Seth running his fingers through it.

"Come on, Diogee, let's go see if we've got any eggs for breakfast," Hannah beckoned the aging rott-weiler sleeping on her feet.

The morning air already held the promise of another unseasonably warm day. November, and the thermometer was still reaching into the high seventies. Hannah tossed several handsful of feed onto the ground before scurrying into the chicken coop to search through the straw for fresh eggs. It wasn't that she was necessarily a coward, but the task was much easier when the chickens were outside.

Normally she didn't mind the daily rituals required

to keep her few animals healthy and productive. When she found the need to flee Albuquerque and the painful memories it held, her grandparents' farm had been the perfect solution. Her grandfather had died five years ago and Granny could no longer maintain the property. Once Hannah agreed to accept the responsibilities of owning the first farm in Hanson County, Granny had checked into Sunset Acres with all the haste of a newlywed.

Hannah normally enjoyed the independence. This morning, however, she had the distinct impression someone was staring over her shoulder. She had tried to convince herself she was being silly, but she couldn't resist the urge to double check every nook and cranny of the farm yard. And then there was the matter of the disappearing cheesecake.

"What is it, boy?" Hannah reached down to pet the stout neck of the growling dog beside her. Diogee had been a present from Seth on their first anniversary. Ten years later he was still her constant companion and all she had left of her husband. "Probably just a pheasant. Go get it!"

Diogee took off for the small patch of corn growing to the south of the house. Within seconds his fierce growl became a startled whine and Hannah felt the fine hair on the back of her neck stand up. Dropping the egg basket, she flew up the steps of the back porch and into the pantry off the kitchen.

When Seth entered law enforcement, he forced her to learn to use safely the many guns he had in the house. She tried to share his passion, but her interest in guns had only been a feeble attempt to forge the weakening bond between them. It was times like this, being alone so far from town, she was glad for the knowledge. Quickly sliding the shells into the shotgun, Hannah retraced her steps until she stood in plain view of the cornfield. "If anyone's there, come on out."

A rustle in the tall grass was her only answer. "Diogee, come, boy."

The large black dog made his way out of the dying stalks, the hairs along the back of his neck still standing on end. He cast one last glance at the cornfield and obeyed his mistress.

Hannah grimaced against the weight of the gun. She hadn't practiced since Seth's death and the weapon was uncomfortable in her hands. "If you know what's good for you, you'll get the heck off my land." Hannah surveyed the surrounding outbuildings, perfect hiding places for the transients who wandered off the main highway. "I've called the sheriff."

Diogee balked at being pulled back into the house, but Hannah didn't want him out there alone. It was silly, but the dog was really too old to be any protection and she couldn't bear the thought of anything happening to him.

"Eli . . ." She spoke quietly into the kitchen phone after punching a number. "I think someone's messing around the cornfield."

After a few quick words the line went dead and she knew he was on his way. The best thing about having the local sheriff as a best friend was fast service. She made a hurried dash through the house checking the locks. Years of living with a lawman had taught her the need for safety. She slid the dead bolt on the back door and sat at the kitchen table to wait for Eli.

Twice this week she thought she heard someone moving around the property at night. She finally decided it was coyotes and then the cheesecake disappeared. Eli was convinced Diogee was the culprit, but Hannah knew the dog didn't care for sweets, especially not a double chocolate cheesecake with fudge sauce. And while Hannah thought Diogee was the most brilliant animal alive, even she was hard-pressed to believe he could open the refrigerator door.

No, something odd was going on around the property. The sound of running water would awaken her in the middle of the night. She caught a whiff of an odd scent every now and then as she walked through the house. Some internal female instinct told her she was not alone. And it ticked her off.

She gave serious consideration to marching into the cornfield and provoking a confrontation with whatever or whomever was out there. Years ago, when she had been younger and sure of the future, she wouldn't have been so brave. Now she knew the future was only an illusion. Today was reality, tomorrow only a fantasy of what might never be.

A soft clinking in the basement jarred her from her morbid philosophizing and she crossed the kitchen to press her ear against the door. Another clink. Someone or something was in the basement. Her ire rose at the thought of them actually entering her home.

It took all of her one hundred and twenty pounds to drag a protesting Diogee to the pantry and lock him in. Hannah silently slid open the basement door. Her privacy had been invaded, she couldn't afford to wait for Eli. No, make that *wouldn't* wait.

A faint mustiness teased her nose as she made her way down the wooden steps to the basement. She hadn't been down here in a few days and already a spider had stretched his web across the stairway. Using the tip of the gun barrel, she tore through the delicate threads and cautiously stepped down into the darkness.

The light switch was at the bottom of the stairs and she cursed the fact she still hadn't bothered to rewire it. She must be crazy slinking around here in the dark. A fine sheen of moisture covered her palms, making the shotgun slip dangerously in her grip. Only a few more steps and she would be at the light switch. She wiped her palms along jean-clad thighs and adjusted her grip on the gun, wanting to make sure she had the advantage.

The hard rock of the wall scratched her knuckles as her fingers scrambled for the switch. A mild click and the basement was flooded with light. Squinting against the glare, she planted her feet firmly on the bottom step. "Come on out, buster."

For a brief moment only her ragged breath broke the silence. Had she scared him off or was he preparing to make his move? "I know you're down here."

"Hello, Hannah." The soft voice pierced the fear swirling in her mind, turning it to pure terror.

Hannah whirled in the direction of the voice, her eyes widening in disbelief as she stared at the man in front of her. "Dear Lord," she managed to whisper before the floor began to spin, dragging her down into oblivion.

Kane grabbed the shotgun with one hand and Hannah with the other, laying them both gently at his feet. He wasn't surprised at her reaction to seeing him. It had to be a pretty frightening experience finding a dead man in your basement. "Hannah, wake up."

His fingers brushed along the delicate skin of her cheek, glancing over the fullness of her lips and tracing the outline of her ear. Funny, he hadn't realized how beautiful she would become.

A noise in the kitchen brought him from his memories and flipping off the light, he quietly made his way to the hidden corner of the basement. He wasn't quite ready to explain his presence.

"Hannah!" A man's voice bellowed down the stairs. From his hiding place Kane could see Hannah begin to stir.

"Eli!" she called, her voice husky with fear. "I'm down here."

Within seconds a large, black-haired man was scooping Hannah into his arms and carrying her up the steps. Kane's jaw twitched at the unexpected discomfort he experienced at seeing her in another man's arms. What the hell was wrong with him? That was his brother's wife!

Sweet little Hannah. Not so little anymore. Was she still as sweet? Damn, he didn't want to think about it.

He could still remember the way his breath caught when Seth brought her home from college that first Thanksgiving. She had been the epitome of a college co-ed and everything he didn't need. Long legs encased in skin tight jeans topped by an oversize sweatshirt proclaiming her choice of sorority. Her soft brown hair pulled back in a ponytail and a creamy complexion covered with a smattering of freckles hadn't begun to indicate the beauty of Hannah, the woman.

She punched through his carefully cultivated hardness to pierce the vulnerable softness he tried so hard to eradicate. A DEA agent had no room for vulnerability. When he found himself touched by her innocence, he barricaded himself behind harsh words and abrupt actions. Anyone else would have been put off by his attitude, but Hannah persisted in casting him a quick smile whenever she passed him in the hallway of his parents' home. It wasn't until the day after Thanksgiving that he finally found a way to alienate her.

Seth was playing basketball with a high school friend while his parents took his grandmother to the cemetery to visit his grandfather's grave. Hannah, thinking she was alone, traipsed down the stairs in what barely passed for a nightgown. With all that hair tumbling around her shoulders and her soft brown eyes still drowsy from sleep, she was walking temptation. Too much of one for a grown man who hadn't had any sleep due to those very eyes. Taking her in his arms, he captured her surprised lips with his own and kissed her until he thought they might both melt into the linoleum.

"Come back when you grow up," he whispered against her ear and felt her stiffen under the intended insult. He watched her stomp out of the kitchen and hadn't seen her again until the day before she married his brother.

Now, ten years later, his brother had been murdered and the man responsible was after the widow. The only thing standing between Hannah and the drug dealer's revenge was Kane. A man who had been dead for eight years.

TWO

"Hannah?" Eli carefully laid his burden on the over-stuffed sofa in the living room of the small farmhouse. "Junebug, what happened?"

"Kane!" Hannah pushed Eli's hand off her forehead and sat up. *Dear Lord, had she really seen Kane McCord in her basement?*

"What are you talkin' about, honey?" The lines around Eli's mouth deepened with his scowl. "You said something about a prowler."

Hannah laid her head against the back of the sofa and tried to corral her thoughts. Had it been a figment of her imagination or was he real? Maybe it was a doppelganger?

"A what?" Eli's startled expression made her realize she had spoken her thoughts out loud. "I hope that's not as bad as it sounds."

"I was just talking to myself," she explained, embarrassment highlighting the high cheekbones of her heart-shaped face. "A doppelganger is like a ghost. A double image."

18

Eli nodded as if Hannah had suddenly declared herself the Empress of France and he was merely trying to pacify her until help arrived. "Sounds reasonable."

"Oh, it does not!" Hannah pushed herself up off the couch and began pacing from the rocking chair to the woodbox and back again. Having known the sheriff since they were seated next to each other in kindergarten, she counted him as her best friend. How would he react to her . . . her what? Vision? Hallucination?

"Does this dopplewhatsis have anything to do with why you called me?" Eli eased back onto the couch, prepared to wait until Hannah came up with her answers.

"Sort of," she admitted, sinking down into the ancient oak rocking chair next to the fireplace. She felt a little tremble at the intensity of his gaze and knew nothing less than the truth would satisfy him. "I think I saw Kane McCord in my basement."

Eyebrows raised, Eli leaned forward, resting his elbows on his knees. "Seth's brother? I thought he was dead."

Hannah nodded. A wisp of light-brown hair fell into her eyes and she retied the ribbon at the base of her neck. "That's what we were told. He died in a plane crash in California over eight years ago."

Eli pursed his lips before continuing. "Are you telling me you've seen a ghost? Shoot, Hannah, that's a matter for the preacher, not the sheriff."

Hannah rolled her eyes and buried her face in her hands. "I don't know what I saw," she admitted and explained about her trip to the basement.

"Damn, Hannah, you know better than to go off on your own." Eli was more troubled by Hannah's foolish behavior in confronting a prowler than her possible ghost sighting. "You knew I was on my way."

"But what about Kane?" Hannah refused to argue about her right to protect her property. "Have I lost my mind?"

Eli strode across the room and pulled her into his arms. "No, honey. I'll bet it was just stress. Have you been thinking about Kane lately?"

"Not especially, why?" She answered quickly. Her thoughts of Kane had always been a private issue, one she didn't share, not even with Eli.

"Just thought that might be what conjured up this doppledohicky." Eli eased her back into the rocking chair and flipped the snap on his holster. "You stay here. I'll go check it out."

"No!" Hannah grabbed his arm before he could leave. "There's nothing down there. I was just acting like a Nervous Nellie."

"Still," Eli reasoned, "I'd feel better."

Hannah shrugged, knowing it was futile to argue with him. Eli had been looking out for her since Joe Bob Bradly pushed her down in the playground. He considered it his sacred duty to make sure Hannah was happy. "Check then. I'll start us some breakfast."

After letting Diogee out of his prison, Hannah remembered the eggs scattered on the lawn. Eli would be expecting a homemade breakfast, not stale cereal out of a box. That was *her* sacred duty—making sure bachelor Eli got at least one home-cooked meal a day.

Luckily a few eggs had managed to stay intact and Hannah set about whipping up a western omelet while Eli poked through the shelves in the basement. "Hear any chains rattling?" Now that she was up in the clear morning light, it was easy to joke about her specter.

"Very funny." Eli closed the door behind him and tossed his Silverbelly Stetson on the counter. "I left the light on. Don't go down there unless it's absolutely necessary. I'll send Floyd over to rewire that light."

Hannah accepted Eli taking over with only a fleeting thought that she should tell him to mind his own business. He wasn't doing a thing she hadn't planned on doing herself and an argument wouldn't solve anything. Eli was having a difficult time adjusting to the new Hannah. "Thank you."

"I'm being bossy again, huh?" Eli ducked his head, waiting for her reaction. The concern in his warm brown eyes made it impossible for her to be angry. He was her friend, her protector, and the shoulder she cried on.

"Yes, but don't worry about it." Hannah topped off his coffee cup and added another slice of toast to his plate. "It's my own fault. I've let you take care of me for too long."

"I want to take care of you, Junebug," Eli assured, his voice husky as he used her old nickname.

"I have to learn to do things for myself," Hannah reasoned; her eyes begged for his understanding. She wouldn't hurt this dear man for anything, but it was time she started taking responsibility for herself. "I've been depending on you entirely too much lately. I'm a big girl, I need to know I can depend on *me* for a change."

"I'll try, honey, but it's gonna be hard," Eli admitted.

"On both of us." Hannah laid her hand across his and the two friends shared a special smile. "Ever since the day Joe Bob Bradly shoved me in the sandbox, you've been fighting my battles."

"Just don't get too independent on me." Eli finished off his coffee and grabbed an extra piece of toast as he headed for the door. Standing in the doorway, the sunlight against his back, he was an imposing figure. From the toe of his heavily scuffed boots to the brim of his cowboy hat, there was no doubt as to his origin or occupation. Eli Gunn had practically been born a sheriff. And like for any good lawman, it wasn't merely a job, but part of who he was. A part Hannah understood better than most. "There's not much to keep me busy in Hanson."

Long after she should have been about her chores, Hannah sat at the kitchen table wondering about the course her life had taken. When she married Seth McCord she pictured a future full of children and growing old together. A bullet shattered that picture. Her life stretched before her like an empty canvas waiting for her to add form and color. Except she always painted by the numbers and had no idea what to do with this freedom. There was no one there to hold her hand and guide her strokes.

By the time Hannah eased her white cotton baby-doll nightgown over her head that night, she had worked herself almost to the point of exhaustion. After Eli left she finished her normal routine and then some. In the weeks following Seth's death she learned hard work, lots of it, was the only way she would sleep through the night. It had been months since she found it necessary to employ the tactic.

Running a brush through her hair, she quickly plaited it into a thick braid before sliding between the cool sheets and switching off the light. Her bedroom was instantly bathed in the glow of the full moon hovering just outside her window. The branches of the ancient elm tree in the front yard cast eerie, gnarled shadows on the wall and Hannah's thoughts immediately flew to her ghost theory.

Had her guilt conjured Kane's image? Was she being punished for sharing a life with one man while being in love with his brother? "Diogee, I think I'm going around the bend."

The rottweiler raised his head off her feet and stared at her for a brief second before rotating his large frame into a more comfortable position on the foot of her bed. Diogee had seemed like the perfect bed partner once she found she couldn't sleep alone. Much better than Joe Bob Bradly or one of the other locals who had begun asking her out with irritating regularity.

When she had returned to Hanson, the locals had respected her mourning. Then about a year after the accident, Hannah found herself in the unenviable position of being the "prize catch." Granted there were only a handful of single women in the sparsely populated county, but Hannah's interest in men rated about the same as a case of smallpox.

Unfortunately, no one, not even Eli, understood her desire to remain alone. She had been fixed up, tricked, and threatened by just about everyone she knew. "Maybe when they hear I've lost my mind, they won't be so interested."

Diogee grunted his disapproval at her late-night conversation and she indulged in the childish act of sticking out her tongue. Reaching over, she ruffled the thick fur on his neck. "Some help you are."

Hannah snuggled deeper under Grandma Sandeson's quilt listening to the comforting sounds of the old farmhouse settling down for the night. The soft hiss of the wall furnace in the hallway turning off and on, the creak of the clapboards contracting with the night chill, the gentle pop of the refrigerator door opening. *The refrigerator door opening?* "Diogee?"

A soft, reassuring snore came from the other side of the bed. What good was a watch dog that would rather sleep than attack? "Diogee." Her voice was barely more than a harsh whisper, but she easily detected the terror underlying her words. Someone was downstairs rummaging through her kitchen.

Slipping her feet into tattered slippers too comfortable to throw away, Hannah silently made her way from the bedroom to the top of the stairs. What kind of burglar made himself a midnight snack? *The kind that looks for jewelry in the freezer.*

Grabbing her grandfather's ornately carved walking stick from the upper hall closet, she crept down the stairs, finally coming to a stop just outside the kitchen door. There was no way of knowing what she would discover once she crossed the threshold. A robber, a bum, Kane's ghost.

The light from the open refrigerator slanted its glow across the black-and-white checks of her kitchen floor. It also clearly outlined a large man helping himself to her freshly cooked Virginia ham and a beer. Hannah stood for a long moment studying the muscles of his broad back as they bunched and stretched to accommodate his movements. He bent over to retrieve a wheel of cheddar and she was witness to the perfection of his backside, neatly encased in jeans that had seen better days.

"Don't forget the mustard." *What else did one say to a midnight burglar?*

The man dropped the large platter of meat to the

floor, sending slivers of china and ham across his boot-clad feet and onto the newly scrubbed linoleum. Diogee's startled bark carried down the stairs, followed by the rapid thud of his heavy paws making their way toward the kitchen. "Hell, Hannah, don't do that."

Don't do that? She was scared out of her wits and all this refrigerator-raiding ghost had to say was "Don't do that?" Shaking her head at the absurdity of her situation, she raised the heavy wooden cane high enough for her visitor to become aware of it. "Kane McCord, I don't know why you've suddenly decided to haunt me, but I don't like it."

"Hannah, put down the stick and let's talk." Kane's voice was reassuring. He took his gaze off hers for a split second to eye the large dog standing beside her. "Hi there, boy."

Hannah watched his eyes travel the length of her scantily clad body. Why couldn't she ever remember to put on a robe? "You're dead."

"I think I probably have some explaining to do." Kane scooped up the largest pieces of the shattered platter and tossed them into the wastebasket next to the back door. Diogee seemed to be reassured Hannah was in no danger and began helping himself to the ruined ham.

Hannah watched as he set about the mundane task. It certainly didn't strike her as something a ghost would do. As a matter of fact, Kane didn't seem to possess any unearthly qualities. He wasn't transparent and he didn't moan, but then neither had Patrick Swayze in *Ghost*. Of course, Whoopie Goldberg had only been able to *hear* Patrick, no one had been able to see him . . . What was she doing? This was real life, not the movies.

"Why are you here?" Her voice caught slightly and she cleared her throat before trying again. "Do you have some message for me?"

A chuckle echoed deep in his chest. "Hannah, I'm real. I'm just as real as you are." He held out his hand but stopped just short of touching her. "I'd feel much better if you'd drop the club."

She glanced up at the forgotten cane and cautiously lowered it to her side. "I don't understand."

Kane switched on the kitchen light and they both blinked against the sudden intrusion. "Sit down. You need something to drink. Whiskey?"

"Tea." Sinking into the nearest kitchen chair, she barely managed a whisper. Was this how it happened for most people when they went insane? Did they find themselves talking to ghosts in their kitchen at two o'clock in the morning? "I thought you just heard voices in your head telling you to eat dirt or fly off a building."

"What?" Kane glanced up from his chore, blue eyes filled with confusion.

Hannah raised her shoulders slightly. "I didn't realize all this happened when you lost your mind. Will I still see you when they lock me up?"

"Hannah, sweet Hannah." Kane set the tea kettle on the stove and quickly lit the flame under it. "Baby, you aren't losing your mind. I'm not a ghost."

"But you're dead," she reasoned, flinching as he stood next to her. "I went to your funeral."

The tips of Kane's mustache tilted up in a rakish air Hannah remembered too well. "How was it?"

"Fine." Hannah smiled. She supposed it was a reasonable question. "The church was full and there wasn't a dry eye in the place by the time Mr. Peabody finished the eulogy.''

"Mr. Peabody, my old English teacher?" Kane jerked the whistling kettle off the stove and filled two cups with steaming water. "I thought he hated me?"

"Well, it's easy to say nice things about a person after they're dead." She accepted the offered teacup, wincing as the china burned her fingers. Taking a small sip, she savored the sweet tea before raising her eyes to the man sitting across from her. Was it really Kane? Although his skin was darker and there was something wrong with the shape of his face, the eyes couldn't belong to anybody but a McCord. "What happened to your face?"

Kane opened the back door at Diogee's insistence, before answering. "Plastic surgery."

"What?" His answer took her by surprise and she choked on her tea. Coughing up the offending liquid, she stared at him through teary eyes.

"Hannah, the plane crash was a ruse." Kane's voice belied his reluctance. "Too many people were looking for ways to get to me. The family was in danger. I had to go under."

"You mean underground?" A faint glimpse of understanding sparkled in the recesses of her mind. "Like a witness protection program?"

"In a way," he agreed. Reaching across the table, Kane traced the delicate line of her jaw. "I couldn't take the risk of someone getting hurt."

"But someone did." The small flicker of life shining in Hannah's eyes died. "Seth got hurt."

"I know." His whispered words rang through the kitchen.

Hannah's fingers gripped the edge of the table as she

rose to tower over him. "Seth's dead and it's all your fault!"

Kane watched as Hannah grabbed her stick and opened the back door. Without another word, she fled from the kitchen. He longed to go after her but some shred of remaining wisdom told him now was not the time. She was still suffering from the shock of finding out he was alive. There would be plenty of time to settle matters. He wasn't going anywhere until Hannah was safe from Sanchez.

Flinging the remains of his tea into her pristine white sink, he strode to the cabinet over the refrigerator. He found Hannah's meager liquor supply the first night he hid out in her basement and right now he needed something a hell of a lot stronger than cinnamon-apple spice tea. Foregoing the use of a glass, he tipped the bottle of Southern Comfort to his lips and let the liquid burn a path down his throat. Sure he could protect her from Sanchez, but who was going to protect her from him?

THREE

Diogee nuzzled her chin before sliding his tongue over her face in an effort to awaken her. "Leave me alone."

Desperate to escape the confines of the room, the dog proceeded to bound from the bed to the door and back, whining with each step. "Okay, I get your point."

Testing the air with one foot, Hannah decided to brave the early-morning chill and forced herself upright. Her eyes were sandy from lack of sleep and her jaw muscles ached from grinding her teeth. Not bothering with her robe or slippers, she padded down the stairs to let Diogee out for his morning run.

Sunlight filled the kitchen and she realized it was long past six o'clock. "We overslept, Diogee." The dog was waiting impatiently by the back door and Hannah hurried to let him out. "Sorry, boy."

The smell of coffee filled the kitchen and she silently thanked Eli for the automatic coffee maker he gave her last Christmas. She was a woman of few vices, but she refused to give up her coffee. "Ahh."

"Dammit, Hannah!" Kane's voice shattered the quiet morning air and Hannah's full cup of coffee hit the floor with a dull thud before splashing the hot liquid over her feet and ankles.

"Ow, shoot." Jumping away from the large brown puddle, she stared at him. "What is the matter with you?"

"Get upstairs and put on some clothes." Kane indicated her uncovered nightie before grabbing a tea towel from the drawer.

By the time he wiped the coffee off the floor she was gone. He hadn't meant to shout at her, but the sight of her standing there with the morning sun highlighting each luscious curve through the thin cotton nightgown was more than he could handle. The scene was too reminiscent of that morning in his parents' kitchen. "Get a grip, McCord, she's Seth's wife."

"No, I'm not," Hannah said from the doorway of the kitchen. Tucking her red flannel shirt into her blue jeans, she walked across the kitchen to stand in front of him. "I'm Seth's widow. And you're his dead brother."

"I'm not dead, Hannah." Kane picked up the heavy braid of hair hanging over her shoulder and tugged. "Trust me."

Reading the tension in his blue eyes, Hannah nodded and moved to the other side of the table. "This is all too strange, Kane. Why are you here? Why now?"

The sound of a gunshot echoed through the morning air, sending Kane across the table, knocking Hannah to the floor beneath him. "Get down."

"Kane, what was that?" she cried, trying to push herself up. "It sounded like a gun."

"It was," he confirmed, and shoved her head under his shoulder while reaching for his ankle holster. "Stay down."

"Do I have any choice?" she muttered into his shirt.

"No." He slid them under the heavy oak table and told her with his eyes not to move. Inching his way across the cool floor, he tried to gauge the direction of the shot. Damn, what kind of protection was he going to be if he couldn't keep his mind on the job? One look at the woman and he had all but forgotten Sanchez and the threat to Hannah.

The muffled sound of an engine being started caught his attention and he dared a peek out the kitchen window. A plume of dirt rose from the road leading to the highway and he hurried to unlock the door. "Stay there."

Hannah watched Kane slide the dead bolt open and slip outside. "Kane, wait, it's only a hunter." She was almost to the kitchen door when she heard it. A low, keening wail much like that of an injured animal. *"Diogee!"*

Rushing out the back door, Hannah was caught up against Kane's broad chest. "I told you to stay put."

"Let me go." Breaking free of his grip, Hannah hurried across the yard toward the outbuildings. "Diogee."

A pained whimper carried her to the smallest barn. "I'm coming, baby."

She barely reached the half-open door before Kane caught her in his arms, pulling her to the ground. "Are you trying to get yourself killed?"

"Let me go," she cried, pushing against him. "Dio-gee's hurt."

"And you're gonna be dead," he growled, grabbing her flailing arms and pinning her under him. "They might still be out there."

"Who?" Hannah followed Kane's eyes as they surveyed the house and yard. "You mean the hunters? I hope to heck they are."

"Hunters?" Ripping his eyes from the surrounding fields, he stared down into the angry depths of her eyes.

"It's dove and deer season," she pointed out. "I don't allow hunting on my land, but that doesn't always stop them. Now let me up. One of the bastards shot Diogee."

"Okay, we'll check it out, but keep your keister down." He shoved hard on her backside as she crawled along the ground. "I don't want anyone mistaking you for a deer."

Ignoring him, Hannah pulled herself into the building and stood up. "Diogee."

"Hannah?" Kane placed his hands on her shoulders and turned her to him. "Honey, I think you better wait here."

The sudden warmth in his voice sent an alarm off in her head. "Where is he?"

"Let me check him." Pulling her into his arms for a bracing hug, Kane strode across the building. Without much light it was difficult to locate the wounded animal. Kane bit back a cuss word as he finally found him huddled in the far corner. "I found him."

"Is he . . . ?" She couldn't say the word. Wiping her hands on her jeans, she made her way to where Kane knelt.

"No, not yet." Kane held his hand in front of Diogee's nose to let the dog smell the familiar scent. "It's okay, boy, we're gonna get you fixed up. Hannah!"

"I'm right here." Her words were barely more than a choked whisper as she stared at the scene before her. Diogee lay on his side, eyes glazed with pain. He attempted to raise his head at the sound of her voice, but he was too weak. "Where was he shot?"

"In the neck." Kane's voice remained calm and soothing.

"I'll call the vet." Hannah tried to keep the panic from tingeing her words, conscious of the fact that Diogee would respond to her distress. "Stay with him."

"Hannah?" Kane called as she hurried out of the building.

"Yes?" Pushing the door wide open, she caught sight of the anguish written across Kane's face.

"Call the sheriff." He didn't bother to wait for her reply before turning back to Diogee.

Racing across the backyard, Hannah fought the urge to scream her frustration. She was forced to hang up twice before she managed to hit the correct number for Dr. Awbrey. Luckily Eli's number was on her phone memory. "Eli, Diogee's been shot."

"Right." The click of the phone told Hannah he was on his way.

Filling a pan with hot water, Hannah grabbed a handful of dishrags and headed out the door. The phone began ringing but she ignored it. Rushing across the yard to the barn, she made her way to the far corner where Kane sat comforting Diogee. "They're both on the way."

Kane took the wet rag from her and immediately began swiping at the entry wound. "I think the bullet hit his shoulder. Looks like a pretty small caliber."

"You have to stop the bleeding." Hannah reached shaking fingers toward the wound before pulling them back. "Stop the bleeding."

Folding a clean towel, Kane applied pressure to the wound. "How's that?"

"You have to stop the bleeding or Seth will die," Hannah ordered, sitting on the soft pile of straw beneath them. Her body shook as the memory of her husband's death overtook her.

"Hannah?" Kane's eyes found hers and a shudder rippled through him as he watched her mouth move over unspoken words. "Hannah, dammit, hang on. I can't let go or the bleeding will start up again. Hannah!"

"Hannah. Hurry up." Seth stood on the sidewalk, *his hands planted on his hips. "I can't wait to get out of this damned tie."*

"Seth McCord," Hannah giggled, shaking the rocks *from her shoes. "This is our anniversary. Quit hollering at me."*

"I know it's our anniversary, darlin'." He waggled *his eyebrows, a lecherous smile curving his full lips. "That's why I'm in such a hurry to get home."*

"Bull." Hannah replaced the strappy high heel and *started toward her husband of eight years. "You just want to get home and watch wrestling."*

She watched him flex his muscles in a familiar body builder's pose and laughed at the picture he made. The streetlight caught the laughter in his blue eyes as he turned to stroll to the car. It also illuminated the three men as they stepped from behind a black van parked on the curb.

"You should have listened," the largest man sneered

before pulling a small pistol from beneath his jacket and pumping three bullets into Seth's startled body.

"Hannah!" Seth cried as each tiny piece of metal ripped into him, robbing him of his life.

Hannah's feet refused to move as she watched the men casually climb into the van and drive away. For a long second she stood there as if watching a dream. It couldn't be real. "Seth."

Carefully approaching the prone body of her husband, she knelt beside him, half expecting him to roll over and give her his cockeyed grin, the one he always used when he played a trick on her. Except this wasn't a trick.

"Seth!" Frantically pulling his head onto her lap, she pressed her hands against the blood-soaked wound on his chest. "Help me, please. Help me!"

"What's going on in here?" A large white-haired man pushed the door of the building wide open, flooding it with morning light. "Hannah?"

"We're over here," Kane said, hoping this was the vet. He was anxious to hand the dog over to an expert so he could concentrate on Hannah. "Diogee's been shot."

"Good gracious." The elderly man hurried across the building, snapping open his bag. "Get out of my way, young man."

Kane gratefully moved back from the injured animal as the vet set about his task with sure hands and soothing words. "Hannah, you okay?"

Still caught up in the horror of that night, Hannah rocked back and forth, her hands clutching at the straw covering the floor. "Help me."

"She needs some air, Doc." Without waiting for a

reply, Kane lifted Hannah to his chest and carried her out into the sunlight. "Hannah, come on."

Blinking against the light, Hannah stared at Kane through troubled eyes. "Kane? Where's Seth?"

Holding her tighter, Kane willed her to take his strength. Or what was left of it anyway. He could deal with unknown gunmen and injured animals but he was totally unprepared to handle a woman caught up in the horror of a flashback. He had seen enough of them through the years, men who still dreamed of Vietnam or the current war with the equally ruthless drug lords. He had experienced them a time or two after surviving a particularly harrowing bust. No man could pull the trigger on his gun and calmly walk away. It might take a while for it to catch up, but the paralyzing terror of that split second would come back.

"Kane?" Hannah pulled her face from the protection of his shoulder. "I'm gonna be sick."

Helping her to the side of the building, he held her while her body shook itself loose from the terror. Tugging his handkerchief from his back pocket, he offered it to her when the spasms stopped. "You okay now?"

Running the cloth over her ashen face, Hannah nodded. "I need to check on Diogee."

"No." Kane stood in front of the door, his feet planted.

"Let me in there." Hannah pushed against his chest but he didn't budge. "Who do you think you are?"

"Hannah, let the doctor take care of Diogee." Kane grabbed her wrists to keep her from fighting him anymore. "If you don't stop it I'm going to tie you to the fence post over there."

"Let me go!" Hannah begged, trying to tug herself from his grip.

"You heard the lady." The soft voice held a steel edge Kane couldn't deny. "Get your hands off her and put them where I can see them. Hannah, step away from him."

"Eli, it's okay." Hannah rushed around Kane to place a restraining hand on the sheriff. "He isn't hurting me."

"Who the hell is he?" Eli eased his finger from the trigger of his pistol but didn't replace it in his holster. "And where's Diogee?"

"Kane, you can turn around now," Hannah told him. "Eli Gunn, this is Kane McCord."

The lawman eyed him with unconcealed skepticism. "Looks pretty healthy for a dead man."

"He is," Hannah agreed, aware of the tension between the two men. "I mean, he isn't dead. It has something to do with being underground."

"Hannah!" The harsh tone of Kane's voice stopped any more explanations. He didn't know this man, but he supposed the good sheriff was on the up and up. Still, his past was better left unexplained until he could be sure of the lawman.

"Where's Diogee?" Eli repeated, his eyes never leaving Kane.

"I'll show you." Hannah started for the building, but Kane's hand shot out and grabbed her arm. "Kane!"

"He's in there with the vet," Kane told Eli, pulling Hannah toward the house. "We'll be inside."

"Hannah?" Eli's voice told her he would interfere, but only at her request.

"It's okay, Eli." Hannah grimaced at Kane as he pushed her up the steps ahead of him. "Check on Diogee for me and I'll make some fresh coffee." Having lived with a McCord for eight years, Hannah knew when they made up their mind about something, nothing short of a nuclear explosion could change it. "Kane can help me."

Not wanting to argue in front of an audience, Kane followed Hannah into the kitchen prepared for a fight. In his experience, women did not take kindly to being ordered around. "All right, let's have it."

"Have what?" Hannah asked, pulling the coffee filters from the cabinet. "Don't you want coffee?"

"Forget the damn coffee, Hannah." Kane grabbed the thin white papers from her and flung them to the table. "I know you're dying to hit me over the head with that coffeepot, so get on with it."

Hannah stared at him. "I don't know what you are talking about, Kane," she insisted, jamming a filter into the coffeepot and tilting the coffee can over it. "I don't have any reason to be angry with you." Filling the glass pot with water, she dumped it into the coffee maker and flipped on the switch. "You did what you had to do."

"That's right I did," Kane agreed, wondering if she realized she was not making coffee but mud. "I'm trained to take charge in situations like this."

Reaching into the bottom cabinet for cleanser, Hannah began scrubbing the already spotless white porcelain sink. "Of course you are," she agreed, thinking how quickly he reacted earlier. "You're trained to deal with idiots who kill for sport. I'm trained to teach music to six-year-olds." Grabbing the window cleaner she ruthlessly attacked the sparkling windowpane over the sink.

Leaning against the doorframe, Kane watched Hannah scurry about the kitchen attacking imaginary dirt. The helpless anger she was experiencing was normal.

And even if she refused to admit to it, he would be worried about her if this morning's episode hadn't upset her. "Hannah, it's okay to be mad. Hell, I'd like to be out there chasing the SOBs down."

Shoving a bar of soap at him, she pointed to his bloodstained hands and shirt. "Wash, please."

Tugging the bloody T-shirt over his head, Kane walked to the sink and began scrubbing Diogee's blood from him. "Sorry, Hannah."

"For what?" The tone of his voice pierced the wall of self-pity and anger she was quickly erecting. She watched him rub the bar of soap over the clearly defined muscles of his forearms.

"For every damned thing." The slight crack in his voice was Hannah's undoing. With a cry she flung herself into his lather-covered arms. "Aw, hell, baby."

"What kind of monster shoots a dog?" Hannah sobbed against the hard plane of his bare chest. "He's all I've got."

Heedless of the bubbles dripping onto the floor, Kane cradled Hannah to him. "No, he's not, Hannah. You've got me." *Hell, she'd always had him even if she didn't know it.*

As her tears subsided she became aware of the heated flesh beneath her cheek. She could hear the slight thud of his heart and the quick rush of his breath as her fingers accidentally brushed across his flat male nipple. "Do I, Kane?"

His soap-covered finger tilted her chin up and he gazed down into eyes the color of sunlight through honey. The sight of her slightly parted lips was too great a temptation and he gave in to the need to brand her as his woman. Capturing her startled cry with his mouth, he gently caressed her lower lips with the tip of his tongue. "More than you know."

"Hmm?" Shocked by a sudden flash of desire, Hannah didn't realize Kane had pulled back. It was only when he pushed her from him that she opened her eyes. "What's the matter?"

"What's the matter?" Kane carefully removed his hands from her and crossed the kitchen to the back door. "You're my brother's wife, Hannah."

In the emptiness of his leaving, Hannah allowed a tear to drop from her lashes. Lifting a trembling finger to her lips, she whispered, "No I'm not, Kane. Maybe I never was."

"You have left the message?" Roberto Sanchez lifted a delicate china cup to his lips and sniffed at the contents. He glanced at his speaker phone, waiting for a reply.

"Yes, sir." There was a hint of pride mixed in with words. "Unless she's an idiot, she'll understand."

"The McCord woman is no idiot, Tony," Sanchez warned his soldier. "She is a strong woman. It's too bad she has not seen the foolishness of her action yet. Contact me in two days for further instructions."

"Yes, sir."

The line went dead and Sanchez took a sip of his coffee. The McCord woman was proving to be tougher than he had expected. He would have to be clever in his manipulation of her fear. It was too bad he had not seen her in the restaurant parking lot. It would have been much easier to kill her then.

FOUR

"No," Hannah said for the fourth time in as many minutes. She had no intention of being locked away in some safe house for the next three weeks. Why wouldn't they listen to her? Smiling, she calmly added a dollop of whipped cream to the huge slice of fresh apple pie on Eli's plate. "Do you want milk or coffee?"

"Milk," Eli mumbled around his fork before glancing at the angry man sitting across from him. He waited until Hannah disappeared into the kitchen before speaking. "I know, it drives me crazy, too. Hannah thinks she can solve everything by stuffing food down someone. I gained thirty pounds after Seth's, uh, well, anyway, after . . ."

"Murder. You can say the word," Kane assured, still assessing Eli and his place in Hannah's life. He liked the soft-spoken man and suspected Hannah did, too. She could have picked someone unsuitable . . . like him.

"Yeah, well, Hannah likes to feed people." He grinned around another mouthful of the carefully spiced dessert. "Luckily, she can cook like nobody's business."

"Hannah's idiosyncrasies aside . . ." Kane paused to check for Hannah's reappearance. "How do we get her out of here?"

Sliding his empty plate onto the coffee table in front of him, Eli shrugged. "I don't know. Used to be she did everything she was told. But lately . . ." Eli leaned back against the couch and shook his head. "Hell, I can't figure her out."

"Who are you trying to figure out?" Hannah breezed into the room like she hadn't been standing at the kitchen door listening to their every word. Handing Eli a tall, frothy glass of milk, she settled next to him on the couch. "Me?"

She watched the almost imperceptible tightening of Kane's jaw as she curled her bare feet up under her and rested her head on Eli's shoulder. *Jealousy?* She ought to tell him that Eli Gunn's shoulder had seen more than its share of her tears through the years and they had never even dated. Oh, there was that experimental kiss behind her grandfather's barn when they were twelve and she had attended a couple of fraternity dances with him in college, but they didn't count. Of course, Kane didn't know that.

"Junebug." Eli reached up to tug gently on her nose. "Kane's right. You can't stay here."

"It's my home." She moved away from him slightly. "I don't think there is anything to worry about."

"Nothing to worry about!" Kane's shout startled her with its venom. "Are you that stupid?"

"Don't yell at me." She used the "schoolteacher" voice designed to quiet a roomful of rowdy children. Surprisingly, it worked on irate men, too. "I am fully aware of Sanchez and the threat he represents. I know he wants me dead, but I refuse to spend the rest of my life hiding like *I'm* the criminal."

"It won't be for the rest of your life," Kane pointed out. "Three to four weeks at the most."

"How do you know that won't be the rest of my life?" she asked with chilling clarity. The room was mournfully silent as the three digested her meaning. They all knew there were no guarantees. "He has taken so much already." Shiny crystal tears brimmed in her eyes. "How can I let him have any more?"

Kane watched as Eli pulled Hannah into his arms for a hug. *What was it with these two?* "I'm not saying you have to go into hiding, but what's wrong with a little caution?"

"I *am* cautious," Hannah insisted, rising to take the dishes into the kitchen. "Ask anyone. I always wear my seat belt and look both ways before crossing a street. Good grief, I even sniff the milk before pouring it."

"Is she kidding?" Kane marveled after she left the room. "Seat belts? Doesn't she have any idea of what this man will do to keep her from testifying?"

"She did watch him gun down her husband," Eli pointed out. "I think this is all part of that new independence kick she's on."

"Well, she can just get the hell off of it." Kane silently made his way across the living room and through the adjoining dining room on his way to the kitchen. He suspected Hannah had her perfectly shaped little ear pressed against the door. Planting both hands on the swinging door, he shoved. A dull thud came from the other side followed by a pained yelp. "Quit eavesdropping and get out here."

"Don't tell me what to do," came the reply.

"How 'bout I do it for you?" With a minimum of action Kane stepped into the kitchen and hoisted Hannah over his shoulder. He recognized his mistake the instant he turned his head. He hadn't planned to touch her again—ever! Now here he was with her pert little bottom stuck in his face. "Quit kicking."

"Put me down, you horse's patootie." Opening her hand, she reached down and slapped him on the rear. The maneuver had the desired effect and she found herself quickly dumped onto the couch. "How dare you?"

"I dare just about anything I want," he warned. "Remember that."

"Hannah, I really need to get back to the office." Eli didn't bother hiding the grin spread across his handsome features. "I figure you'll be all right with Kane, but call me if you need me."

"Eli!" Having momentarily forgotten the man, she blushed at what he must be thinking. "You don't have to go yet."

"Sorry, darlin', but with Texetta down state at her daughter's, we don't have a dispatcher tonight." Eli settled his hat on his head with practiced movements before offering his hand to Kane. "I'll do some checking and get back to you in the morning."

"Checking on what?" Hannah hurried to Eli's side, determined not to be left out.

"Thanks." Kane returned the handshake, ignoring Hannah. "We'll talk more then."

"Talk about what?" Hannah stamped her bare foot

on the braided rug covering the living-room floor, but it didn't matter. The two men were busy communicating in some truly silent macho way, completely ignoring her.

"Don't lock that yet," Hannah protested as Kane flipped the dead bolt on the front door.

Turning to face her, Kane took a deep breath. "You are to keep this door locked at all times," he ordered in a barely audible voice. "Not that a locked door will keep Sanchez out."

"Then why bother?"

"Honey, you are the only thing standing between him and an acquittal." Taking her by the elbow, he led them back into the living room. "I'm not supposed to know this, but the prosecution hasn't come up with another piece of hard evidence linking Sanchez to Seth's murder."

"What about the gun?" She shivered slightly recalling the sight of the weapon clutched in the lethal hands of Roberto Sanchez.

"Hannah, that gun is in a jillion different parts in just as many different places." His voice softened as he realized how little she truly knew about the man she would be sending to prison. "Sanchez has covered his tracks, you can bet your a— hind end on that. He'll even have a dozen people climb up on that witness stand and swear he was nowhere near that restaurant parking lot."

"That's perjury," she insisted, not ready to give in to his arguments.

Dear Lord, what an innocent. "Hannah, didn't Seth ever talk to you about his job?"

Of course, she wanted to say, but it would be a lie. She had wanted to talk to him about his job, if for no other reason than to have something to share. Being a police officer had been the sole reason for Seth's existence, and no matter how hard she tried, Hannah could never find a way to get his attention. "Seth didn't like to bring the job home with him."

Kane merely raised his eyebrows at her claim, but he didn't call her on the lie. He changed the subject instead. "Do I have to sleep on this couch again?"

The non sequitur caught her off guard and for a half a second she thought he was asking to sleep with her. She spent the other half of the second considering the idea. "There's another bedroom upstairs. I'll put fresh linens on for you."

Kane watched her climb the staircase and fought the need to go after her. He had been battling that particular urge all day. All day, hell. He had been confronting his feelings for her since the day they met. Only the fact that Seth had seen her first kept him from acting on those emotions. Although he hadn't seen her in eight years, she had never been far from his thoughts. Now, instead of the faded memory of a young girl, he was dealing with a flesh-and-blood woman.

After that brief kiss in the kitchen, he had known his desire for her was as great as ever. Even thinking of her as his brother's wife no longer helped. Seth was gone and it was time for Hannah to fill the other side of her bed. It wouldn't be with him, couldn't be, but damn, he wanted it to be.

"Kane." Hannah's voice drifted down the stairs and he was halfway to her before he thought to ask what she wanted.

"I need help with the blankets," she informed him, pointing to the top shelf of the linen closet. "You'll probably need a couple of quilts. The nights are getting pretty cool.''

Kane hoped she was telling the truth. The farmhouse didn't come equipped with a cold shower, and he definitely needed cooling off. "I'll take it from here."

He expected her to protest, but instead she merely handed him the clean sheets and pointed toward the bedroom. "I think I'll take my bath first if you don't mind."

"I usually shower in the morning."

"Sorry about the shower," she called over her shoulder. "I'll spray you with the water hose if you like."

A dimple appeared in Kane's left cheek, a mistake on the part of his plastic surgeon. "Better be careful, little girl, I might take you up on that."

Hannah paused in the bathroom door, the teasing glint gone from her eyes. "I hope you do."

Kane was cheated a reply by the closing door, but then he didn't have any idea what he would have said. What kind of game was she playing? One minute she was as innocent as a newborn babe and the next she was looking at him with such heat he was practically scorched ten feet away.

Taking the sheets, he proceeded to make up the double bed across the hall from Hannah's. He had been sleeping alone for years, so why did it bother him so much now?

Hannah added an extra capful of bubble bath before swishing her hand through the foaming water. The water was good and hot and Hannah knew it would be cool before she had the nerve to leave the safe confines of her bathroom. What on earth had possessed her to say that? What was Kane thinking? *Probably that I'm some love-starved widow desperately in need of a man.*

The thought rankled and she grabbed her braid and quickly pinned it on top of her head. If she got it wet tonight it would still be damp in the morning. She opened the medicine chest over the porcelain pedestal sink and actually picked up the scissors before changing her mind. *One of these days,* she promised. *One of these days I'm going to get up the nerve to cut this stuff off.*

Slipping into the steamy water, Hannah reached for the book she had started a couple of days ago. Seth had always warned her about reading in the tub. He was positive she would fall asleep and drown. It was one of the little things she had begun doing to test her newly forming independence.

Eighteen months ago, she had felt like Rapunzel, locked away in her golden tower, lacking any contact with the real world. Perhaps Seth's life had been so filled with the vileness of humanity that he only sought to shield her, but, in the end, she suffered more for his protection. She had been lost, bewildered, much like she was at this moment.

What was she going to do about Kane? Turn him away, hide her true feelings, or jump his bones? The last thought sent a shiver along her naked flesh and she tossed her paperback into the corner of the bathroom. "Shoot!"

"Hannah, what is it?" Kane's voice came immediately from the other side of the bathroom door.

Her eyes rested on the tarnished knob, half expecting it to turn. Her mind raced to think of an answer. "I . . . uh . . . forgot the animals."

"I'll do it," he offered and waited while she told

him precisely what needed to be done. "I'll be back in a few minutes. Where is your extra key?"

"Kane, don't be ridiculous," she protested. "No one is going to break in while you're in the barn."

"The key, Hannah." His voice held a false ring of patience.

"On the treble clef key ring by the back door."

She listened to the solid thump-thump of his boots hitting the stairs before pulling the plug and stepping onto the bath mat. Why did men always have to get their way? Just once she'd like to have the backbone to come away the victor in one of these little battles of the sexes.

The banging of the back door a few minutes later told her Kane had either finished the chores in half the time it would have taken her or he had given up. Either way, it was enough to tick her off.

Peering into the empty hallway, she hurried to her bedroom. In her rush to escape Kane in the small confines of the extra room she had forgotten to take her nightgown and robe into the bathroom. The fact she couldn't traipse around half naked anymore was just another gripe to add to the list.

"Anything else?"

Startled, Hannah spun around and almost collided with Kane as he stepped into her bedroom. "What are you doing in here?"

"I asked if there was anything else you needed me to do." He lowered his voice and reached for the satin lapels of her hastily donned bathrobe.

Thinking he meant to pull her to him, Hannah felt a sharp pang of disappointment when he only tugged the front of her robe closed and quickly tied the belt at her waist. "No."

"No *what,* Hannah?" A sad little smile showed off his dimple as he stepped from her.

No what? "Uh, no there isn't anything else to do." She stammered, staring at the snag marks his calloused fingers left on her robe.

"Did I do that?" he asked, pointing to the marred material.

"Your hands are rough." She took one of his up-turned hands in hers, tracing the coarse flesh with her own soft fingers.

"I live a rough life." He pulled his hand from hers, shoving it into the back pocket of his jeans. "We'd better get some sleep."

"Do you want me to wake you before I leave in the morning?" She sat on the edge of her bed and flipped the switch on her alarm clock.

"You're not going anywhere tomorrow." Striding across the room, Kane pushed the button down on the top of the clock.

"I most certainly am," she insisted, flipping the switch again. "I have a job, you know."

"Call in sick." Once more, the button was shoved down.

"I will not." Another flick.

"Hannah." Down.

"Kane." Flick.

"Damn you're stubborn." He crossed his arms over his chest when she placed a protective hand over the alarm.

"Hah, that's rather like the pot calling the kettle black." Her pulse raced with the exertion of a good argument and she relished how very alive she felt at that moment.

"Fine," he said through clenched teeth. "But I'm

coming with you," he finished quickly, wiping the smug look of victory off her face.

"You can't."

"I am."

Shrugging her shoulders, she decided to call it a draw. "Suit yourself. Just don't blame me if you're bored silly."

"I won't be," he assured her and bent over to place a gentle kiss on her forehead. "See you in the morning."

Hannah listened as he set about making himself comfortable in her home. She timed how long he brushed his teeth and tried to figure out what else he was doing in her ultrafeminine bathroom. "Do you need anything?"

"Yeah, hand lotion," came the muffled reply.

A sweet warmth curled through her at the thought of him applying lotion to his work-roughened hands for her. "It's in the medicine cabinet."

"Thanks."

Within minutes Kane had finished his nightly ritual and the house was dark except for the occasional flicker of moonlight through the clouds. Had it only been twenty-four hours since she found him raiding her refrigerator?

"What am I going to do, Diogee?" She asked before remembering the rottweiler was recovering at the vet's. Reaching over to caress the empty space beside her, she gave in to the tears she had fought all day. Independence was great, but sometimes a woman just needed a good cry.

FIVE

"Hannah!" Kane's bellow jerked her out of a sound sleep and for a second she wondered if she had imagined the roar. Then it came again. "Hannah, get in here!"

Flipping back the covers and forgetting her robe in the process, she hurried into the hallway. "What's wrong? Is it Sanchez?"

"Look at me," he ordered, turning around in the tiny bathroom to give Hannah a good view of his half-nude body.

"My gosh, what happened?" Hannah reached a tentative finger toward his rusty-orange pectoral muscle, delighting when it quivered under her touch.

"That's what I want to know." He pushed his bright-orange hands under the steamy gush of water in the sink and began scrubbing. The water took on a faint bronze tint and Hannah burst into laughter at the sight.

"What did . . . you . . . ." She tried to speak but her words couldn't find room among her giggles.

"Do you suppose this is some kind of allergic reaction to those damn carrots you made me eat yesterday?" His blue eyes held no hint of humor and the puzzled expression on his gorgeous face only made her laugh harder.

"Get out!" she shouted between giggles, shoving him toward the door. "Hurry before I wet my pants."

Her words had their desired effect and Kane quickly stepped into the hall. "I'd like to know what's so funny. I told you I didn't like carrots."

"It's not the carrots," she assured from behind the closed door, "You have a tan."

"A what?" Holding his hands in front of him, he stared at the bright streaks of burnt orange covering them. "You can't get a tan on your palms."

"You can if you use sunless tanning lotion." Hannah opened the bathroom door and plopped a familiar-looking bottle of lotion into his palm. "See?"

"Natural Wonder Sunless Tanning Lotion," he read in disbelief. "Fool your friends into thinking you spent a week in the tropics." He raised his eyes to hers and she was relieved to find a grin tugging at the corner of his mouth. "What the hell is this stuff?"

"Watch your language," she ordered, taking the bottle from him and tossing it into the ribbon-covered waste basket. "You aren't undercover now."

"Yes, ma'am." He offered a mock bow and held his hands up. "What do I do about this?"

"You sit in the bath tub and scrub." She settled her trim figure on the edge of the claw-footed tub and adjusted the temperature of the water. Drawing a man's bath held a strange appeal and she resisted the urge to offer to scrub his back. "It won't all come off, but it'll help."

"Couldn't hurt," was his reply as he led her from the room and locked the door. "I'll be down for breakfast in a few minutes."

"I'll be down for breakfast in a few minutes." She silently mouthed the words, heading for her bedroom and not the kitchen. "Who does he think I am? Betty Crocker? Let him fix his own breakfast."

With a minimum of effort she slipped into fresh underwear and pulled a soft yellow turtleneck over her head. Adding a long denim jumper and comfortable loafers, she felt ready to handle four classes of six- and seven-year-olds. Too bad a few layers of clothes couldn't help her deal with the thirty-six-year-old orange man relaxing in her bathtub.

Kane stared down at the dingy water surrounding him and picked up the washcloth again. There was no way he could leave the house looking like this. "There's got to be something in here that will take this stuff off."

Reaching behind him, he searched through the small stash of feminine products Hannah kept. "Deodorant, extra toothbrushes, pink razors?" He held up the delicate plastic disposable razor and grinned. "Lucky razor," he said, thinking where it was destined to glide.

Finally he managed to locate a small can of cleanser and with a shrug, sprinkled a hefty portion over his chest. The harsh abrasive ground into his flesh, but he knew without a doubt that when he was through, he would have returned to his normal color. No such luck.

After using more than half the can of cleanser he had only managed to tone the bright orange down to a dusty bronze. Not too bad as long as he kept his shirt buttoned and his hands in his pockets. Good thing he hadn't rubbed any lotion on his face.

Picking up a bottle, he carefully read every word on the label before squirting a liberal dose of the perfumed lotion into the palm of his hand and swiping at his buffed skin. "I smell like a French whorehouse."

"Been in a lot of those, have you?" Hannah asked as she passed by the open bathroom door on her way down the stairs.

"Enough to know what one smells like," he grumbled after her. "Smart aleck."

"There's some cologne on the top shelf of the linen closet," she called up to him, purposely ignoring his bad mood. She might feel the same way if she woke up orange.

Shoving aside half a dozen rolls of toilet paper and another dozen boxes of tissue, Kane managed to locate a carefully wrapped package that sloshed when he shook it. A feeling akin to trepidation eased into his mind as he pried the tape from the underside of the box. "What's she doing with cologne?"

The box contained a good-size bottle of a rather expensive cologne and Kane debated whether or not to use it. One whiff of his orange, honeysuckle hands decided the issue. So what if she purchased this for some man . . . Seth? Eli? It was his now. "Better."

Loping down the stairs, he expected to find Hannah busy in the kitchen. Empty. So was the rest of the house. The wide-open back door started his temper rising and by the time he found her talking to the chickens, he was in a rage. "What in hell do you think you are doing?"

"I'm feeding the chickens." She held up a bowl of feed as if to offer proof.

"I thought I told you not to go anywhere by yourself." Grabbing her arm he pulled her into the relative safety of the barn. "Sanchez could be out there right now."

"I checked around." She pulled her arm from his grasp and started back outside. "Besides, I brought this with me." Reaching into the pocket of her jumper, she pulled out a large silver whistle and proceeded to fill the morning air with a shrill tune.

"Hannah!" he warned, following on her heels. "This isn't funny. This is your life we are talking about."

Spinning on her heel, she crashed into his oncoming chest. "That is right, buster!" Stepping back slightly, she stabbed her fingertip in the general vicinity of his face. "*My life*. Not yours. Not Eli's. Mine." Hefting the feed bowl onto her hip, she squinted against the morning sun. "If I want to feed my chickens in the morning, I will. If I want to do my job, I will. Heck, if I want to strut buck naked down Main Street, I'll do that, too."

"That I'd like to see." He grinned at the picture she painted.

"Stick around, buster, and you just might." Flinging the remainder of the feed at the squawking birds, she left Kane standing in the middle of the yard.

Hannah peered through the kitchen curtain to make sure Kane was still standing where she left him before giving in to the need to raise her hands in triumph. She had done it! Outtalked and outmaneuvered Mr. Kane McCord. It was a small victory to be sure and one that probably wouldn't amount to a hill of beans in the long run, but right now she felt ready to take on every male chauvinist in Hanson County.

Hannah felt an odd lump in her throat as she glanced at the two coffee cups resting together on the counter. It was odd having someone to share her mornings with, even if they did spend most of their time arguing. She had been appalled to find out Kane had spent the last week living in her basement. He had been the one to eat the cheesecake and it was his scent that tickled her nose. She had been furious with him for sneaking around and scaring ten years off her life. In typical McCord fashion, he exclaimed it was better than the alternative. Sanchez would do much more than simply scare her. Not that he wasn't doing a good job of that.

On impulse she flipped open the latch on her brief-case and held up the envelope that had arrived in yesterday's mail. Her full name was neatly printed on the face of the pale brown paper. Albuquerque, New Mexico, was clearly stamped on the upper right corner. Her fingers opened the flap and withdrew the thin white paper inside.

Old Mother Hubbard went to the cupboard to get her poor doggie a bone.
When she got there, the cupboard was bare, and the poor doggie was DEAD.

It didn't rhyme. It didn't have to. The message was clear. The events of yesterday morning had been no accident. Someone had taken the time to mail her this poem from Albuquerque to let her know she was being watched. Or was *stalked* a more appropriate description? It should have frightened her. Instead it made her mad.

Hannah knew she'd better hurry if she wanted to sneak off before he started hassling her about staying at home again. She couldn't miss work and there was no way he was tagging along. Hanson was a small town and she was positive everyone already knew a man was living at her place. She hoped people would believe the story Kane and Eli had concocted to explain his presence.

When she had returned to Hanson after Seth's death, she had discovered that her life was general knowledge in town. Not only did everyone in town know about her husband's tragic death, they knew about her honeymoon trip to Hawaii and the fact that the junior high choir she taught had been honored by the governor. They also knew her brother-in-law was "killed" eight years ago. Eli decided Kane should be an old friend in need of a job.

Hannah merely shrugged her shoulders when the two men would ask for her input. So far they hadn't listened to one word she had said.

"You want me to start breakfast?" Kane called from the kitchen just as Hannah picked up her purse.

"Great," she hollered to cover the sound of the front door popping open. "I like my eggs over easy and my bacon crisp. I'll be down in a second." She actually went through the motions of stomping up the first few stairs before sneaking out the front door, leaving it open behind her.

Luckily she had parked along the front of the house instead of her normal spot out back. By the time Kane heard the engine, she would be on her way. "I hope."

Sure enough, she caught a glimpse of him sprinting across the backyard and jumping over the white picket fence just as she turned out onto the driveway. Resisting the urge to stick her hand out the window and wave, Hannah concentrated on ignoring the scowl plastered across Kane's face as he realized she was gone and there was no way he could catch her. "Sorry, Kane, but it is my life."

The morning was rich with the sights and sounds of a new day and Hannah rolled down her window to catch the freshness in the air. The sky was a pale-blue canvas stretched from east to west with only a slight smattering of wispy white clouds and Hannah knew the temperature would again reach record-breaking heights.

Bumping up onto the barely paved farm-to-market road leading to town, Hannah grimaced against the sunlight. In her hurry to escape Kane she had forgotten her sunglasses and made do with her visor. The glare made driving difficult and she slowed down to within a couple of miles of the actual speed limit.

She had two parent-teacher conferences this morning and couldn't afford to be late. Tom Adams had rearranged his schedule to accommodate hers and Letha Thompson was no picnic at any time of the day. The meeting with Tom would be simple enough. His daughter Allison was one of her more gifted students and Hannah felt she ought to have extra training to make the most of her talent. On the other hand, Bradly Thompson's talent lay in making Hannah's life miserable.

Since Letha and Stuart Thompson had separated, Bradly seemed to think he could get away with anything. While Hannah did possess a certain amount of sympathy for the young boy, she wasn't quite ready to hand over her class to his antics. Letha wouldn't want to hear it, but something had to be done about Bradly's anger.

Pulling into her parking space at the school, she glanced at her watch and knew Tom would be waiting for her in the teacher's lounge. She was already several yards away from her car when she remembered she hadn't locked it. Debating for a second, she knew it would be foolish to take a chance. Not that a locked door would make much difference if Sanchez actually wanted her dead, but at least she could assure Eli and Kane that she was taking precautions.

"Hannah!" A tall, gangly man with thinning blond hair stepped out of a muddy pickup truck next to Hannah's and headed in her direction.

With a flick of her wrist, she finished locking the doors and headed toward her old friend. "I figured you'd be pacing the floor waiting for me."

Tom Adams had not altered much since the two had graduated from high school and Hannah was glad. So much had changed in her life that it was reassuring to surround herself with the familiar. "Nah, Allison was in a tizzy this morning 'cause her hair wouldn't work. Danged if I know what to do with her."

Patting his arm as they made their way toward the school building, Hannah grinned. "Don't worry about it Tom. Allison is a perfectly normal twelve-year-old girl and you have done a wonderful job of raising her."

"Sure as heck would be easier if she had a mother," he commented. Being alone in the world was something they both knew about and Hannah didn't feel the need to comment.

Once they were settled in the lounge, Hannah tucked her feet up under her and explained about Allison's unusual talent. "I really think you ought to see about private lessons for her, Tom. She has perfect pitch and can already play the piano by ear. With a little training, there's no telling how far she could go."

"I guess she gets it from her mom. Mary was always

singing around the house. Even at the end . . ." Tom let his mind wander back to better times before the untimely death of his wife six years ago. Hannah let him reminisce for a few minutes before repeating her request for private lessons for Allison.

Tom was agreeable and Hannah promised to find someone equal to the task of molding Allison into a true musical talent. She smiled at the added bounce in Tom's lanky stride as he made his way down the hall. There was nothing quite like finding out other people felt your child was special.

Unfortunately, by the time Letha stomped out of the room, Hannah didn't have the energy to smile. Just as she had suspected, Letha blamed Bradly's problems on her ex-husband and the entire Hanson school system. Letha wouldn't admit there was anything wrong with her child until she was forced to do so and even then she would find someone else to blame.

Sure that the worst was behind her, Hannah gathered her book bag and headed for the music room. The morning kindergarten class was due in twenty minutes and she had to set up. They were studying percussion instruments—always a favorite of five- and six-year-olds.

Inserting her key in the door, she was surprised to find it unlocked. A tremor of anticipation bubbled up her spine as she tugged on the heavy door and reached in to flip on the lights. Was Sanchez or one of his goons waiting for her or had she simply forgotten to lock the door last Friday?

"Where ya been, darlin'?"

"You!" Hannah dropped her bag to the floor with a bang and stood with her hands on her hips facing the man seated in her chair with his boots propped on her desk. "What in heck are you doing here?"

"My job." Kane's voice did not echo the smile on his face. "I thought we agreed I was coming to work with you."

"I don't remember agreeing to any such thing." Hannah flipped his feet to the floor and shoved him out of the way, chair and all. "I seem to recall you mentioning something about it, but I don't believe I agreed."

"You don't have to." With the grace of a panther, Kane swiftly rose from the chair and grabbed her arms. Lowering his eyes to stare into hers, he whispered, "Do you want to die?"

"No." The word was barely audible. Her senses were assaulted by the nearness of the man holding her tightly against his chest. The sight and smell of him sapped her strength, draining the fight from her. "Why would you even ask?"

Kane felt her go limp in his arms and was instantly contrite. "I didn't mean to come on so strong, but . . . Hell, Hannah, you scared the life out of me."

"I didn't mean to." It dawned on her that, despite the circumstances, she was exactly where she wanted to be—in Kane's arms. Taking advantage of the situation, she pressed her cheek to his chest and filled her lungs with his scent. "I just can't let that man take anything else from me."

"I know, baby," he murmured against her hair. "I understand, believe me. But you have to be careful."

"I am." Raising her head, she willed him to see the truth in her eyes. "I don't want to die, Kane. Not when I'm just learning to live again."

An anguished growl echoed deep in his throat before

he brushed his lips over hers. She slid her hands up his chest to wind them in the silver-streaked strands of hair falling over the collar of his navy-blue shirt. When he seemed to be having second thoughts about kissing her, she stood on her toes to press her lips more fully against his, taking the decision from him. "Kiss me."

"I am," he mumbled against her mouth.

"No," she urged. "I mean, really kiss me. The way you did before."

Wrapping her ponytail around his hand, Kane anchored her to him and plunged himself into the ecstasy that was Hannah. Forgetting the danger of their situation and the myriad of reasons he should keep his distance, Kane wallowed in the pure physical and emotional pleasure of the woman in his arms. Twelve years worth of hurt and loneliness went into that kiss and neither one of them heard the muffled giggles of fifteen five-year-olds until Jamie Fuller finally reached up to tug on Hannah's skirt.

"Do we get to learn that today?" the wide-eyed girl asked in all innocence.

SIX

Hannah jumped from Kane's arms and twirled to face their audience. Fifteen pairs of eyes stared up at their beloved Ms. Hannah, awaiting an answer to Jamie's question.

"Is he your husband?" Alex Crownover asked around the thumb shoved in his mouth.

"Ms. Hannah doesn't have a husband," a little girl with an unruly mop of red hair said. "He must be her boyfriend."

"He's too old," a freckle-faced boy without any front teeth commented before grabbing Hannah's hand and pulling her away from Kane. "Who is he, Ms. Hannah?"

"Uh, Devin, he's my . . ." Hannah glanced from the children to Kane.

Squatting down until he was at eye level with the skeptical young man clinging to Hannah's side, Kane held out his hand. "I'm Kane. Hannah's boyfriend."

"Why is your hand orange?"

"Because I put something on it that I shouldn't have," Kane said truthfully, not talking down to the child. "It won't come off."

After a moment's hesitation, the boy returned the handshake. "I'm Devin Anderson. I'm Ms. Hannah's boyfriend, too."

Kane winked. "Think we could share her?"

A smile sprang to Devin's face and he eagerly nodded his head. "We learned about sharing."

"Good deal, partner." Another handshake and the pact was sealed.

"He's cute," Jamie decided suddenly, her tone daring the rest of her classmates to argue. Ever since Jamie had managed to blacken Henry Gonzales's eye during the first week of school, no one dared to dispute her word.

"Come on, kids," Hannah's voice was shaky as she hurried the children to their seats and began explaining the day's activities. Within minutes everyone was banging away on a drum or other percussion instrument. Kane wrinkled his nose, but otherwise kept his mouth shut through three renditions of "Bingo."

It was a constant struggle, but Hannah managed to all but ignore the man sitting in the corner watching her every move. She tried to imagine him not being there, but she was much too aware of his presence to convince herself. By the time she returned the kindergarten class to Ms. Ferguson, Hannah was exhausted. And she still had six hours left before school was out.

"Kane," she said, once the third-graders were through. "I think I'll be fine on my own for a little while. Why don't you go check on Eli?"

"What's wrong with him?" Kane reached up to tuck a stray strand of hair behind her ear.

"I mean, check *in* with him." Ignoring the desire to touch him, she busied herself with a stack of sheet music on her desk. "He was supposed to be talking with the D.A. in Albuquerque about the trial."

"I'm sure he'll let you know when he hears from them." Kane propped his boots on a spare chair and leaned his head against the wall. He resembled the giant elm tree in her front yard—rooted.

"Kane!" Hannah cried. "You cannot sit here all day. I'm sure our kiss is already common knowledge."

"Then what's the problem?" he countered. "If everyone already knows we're having an affair, what harm can I possibly do by sitting here?"

"We aren't having an affair," she reminded him.

"I know that." Suddenly uncomfortable with the conversation, Kane stood and stalked to the middle of the room. With his arms wrapped across his chest, he stared out the window. "But maybe it would be a good idea if the town thinks so. It would be a better explanation than the one Eli and I came up with."

"So, you're saying that we should pretend to be having an affair." For the first time since she found him sitting at her desk, a smile curved Hannah's lips.

"Yeah." Kane didn't take his eyes off the playground located outside the music-room window. "It would explain why we are together all the time, why I'm living with you."

"Do we use your real name?" Although her questions were innocent enough, Hannah's mind was reeling. Would it be possible for either of them to merely *pretend* to be in love with each other? Of course, there would be no need for pretense on her side. She was as in love with him as she had ever been. But what about his feelings for her?

Just when she suspected him of caring, he would withdraw into himself and shut her out completely. Was it possible that she was nothing more to him than simply a protection case? Could he hold her in his arms and kiss her the way he had this morning and not care for her at all?

Her mind ached with the unanswered questions, and she refused to consider it anymore.

"I don't think we'd better do that," he finally answered her. "I'll use Kane, but we'd better go with a different last name. How about Leathers?"

"Kane Leathers." She tried the name on her lips. It didn't have quite the same ring to it, but she guessed it was okay. "I'll try to remember."

"You don't have to." His voice was low as he came to whisper in her ear. "You can just call me lover."

The very thought all but melted her panty hose and Hannah pushed away from him and flew down the hall toward the sanctuary of the ladies' room before she could toss him down amid the bongo drums and have her way with him.

Kalli Johnson was leaning against the bathroom wall with a wet paper towel plastered across her forehead when Hannah rushed through the door. "Whoa. Where's the fire?"

"Kalli," Hannah squeaked. "I didn't see you."

"I'm not surprised." Kalli wet her towel and resumed her position. "You flew through that door like you had a bee in your britches. Hard day?"

"That's putting it mildly." Hannah turned on the cold water and washed her hands before raising her eyes to the mirror. Was her panic that obvious? Did everyone know her secret? Did she have *I love Kane*

McCord tattooed across her face? "This week is always difficult."

"I couldn't agree more." Kalli took a deep breath and tossed her towel in the trash. "I don't know why we even have to come at all. The kids aren't able to concentrate on anything but Thanksgiving."

"I think getting out of school is the main thing." Hannah straightened her shoulders and followed her friend out into the hallway. "I really sympathize with you. They don't seem to mind singing a few songs, but I would hate to be actually trying to teach them something this week."

"That's not what I heard," Kalli teased.

"What?" Hannah dreaded what she knew was coming.

"I heard you found a new way to keep their interest this week." Kalli linked her arm through Hannah's as she teased her good friend. "Something about kissing lessons."

"Oh, no."

"So it *is* true." Kalli tugged Hannah to a halt. "You do have a man in there."

"He's just an old friend," Hannah tried to explain but the look on Kalli's face told her it was useless. "Okay, so he's a very *good* old friend, but I can't get him to leave."

Peering through the small window in the door leading to Hannah's classroom, Kalli whistled. "Get him to leave? You've got to be out of your mind! If he were my old friend, I'd grab the nearest tube of super glue and make him a permanent fixture."

"Hush," Hannah whispered. "He'll hear you."

"So let him," Kalli all but shouted. "If you don't want him, send him down the hall. I'm supposed to be teaching anatomy to my eighth-graders. What a specimen.''

Shaking her head at Kalli as the petite woman affected a rolling stroll down the corridor, Hannah squared her shoulders and vowed she would contain herself around Kane. At least until they got home.

''Hannah!''

Grimacing, Hannah turned to find Mr. Potter, the principal, rushing down the hall. ''Hold up a second.''

''Hi there,'' she smiled, hoping he wasn't going to give her a lecture about having a man in her classroom. If worst came to worst she could always explain about Kane's real reason for being there, but the fewer people who actually knew of the threats, the better. ''What can I do for you?''

''I just wanted to drop off some mail.'' Holding out a large envelope, he waited.

''It's probably just a catalogue, nothing important.'' Shoving the envelope under her arm, she waited to see if any lecture was forthcoming. ''Was that all?''

''Yep.'' He nodded, a glimmer of disappointment flickering in his eyes. ''It was sent special delivery, so I thought it might be important.''

''I'll let you know,'' Hannah promised and entered her room. Even Kane was easier to deal with than Evan Potter. The man took a personal interest in every aspect of his employees' lives and it drove her crazy.

''Feeling better?'' Kane rose from his chair by the window and crossed the room to stand beside her.

''I feel fine.'' Her stomach picked that particular moment to growl, and she grinned. ''Maybe I'm a little hungry.''

''Do you eat in the cafeteria?''

Shaking her head, Hannah dropped the envelope on

her desk and casually tossed a stack of music on top of it. "I usually grab a bite over at Mamie's on Main."

"How about I go pick us up a couple of burgers and bring them back here. I'd rather you weren't out in public any more than necessary."

Raising her eyebrows at his suggestion, she agreed. "That sounds great. You mean you're actually going to leave me alone?"

"I think you should be okay for a few minutes." Kane made a production out of locking the door. "Keep it this way."

"Yes, sir." Hannah offered him a mock salute. Once he was gone she picked up the envelope and held it up to the light as she searched for a postmark. *Hannah McCord, Hanson Independent Schools.* Nothing else to indicate who had sent the letter or where it came from. But she knew. It was from Sanchez. Just like the last one.

Sliding her nail along the glued-back flap, she withdrew the contents. A small photo was attached to a piece of typing paper. Beneath the picture were the words: *"Mary, Mary, quite contrary, How does your garden grow? With silver bells and shotgun shells, Lay them out all in a row."* She stared in horrified fascination at her own image lying in a coffin.

It was time to tell Kane and Eli.

Staring at the envelope in his left hand, Kane bit his lip before giving in to the temptation to call Hannah every vile name he could think of. The list was long and varied, ending with "trusting and innocent"—two attributes he looked on with distaste. He gave serious consideration to packing his bag and heading back to south Texas. Some protection he turned out to be.

"What is wrong with you?" he growled, jerking the paper from her shaking fingers. "I can *not* believe you haven't said something about this before!"

"The last one came from Albuquerque," she reasoned, not really arguing with his assessment of her mental faculties. It *had* been stupid and foolish not to have told him about the first one. Especially after what happened to Diogee. "I wasn't really worried about them until now."

"Why now?"

"No postmark." She pointed to the blank space where there should have been stamps and a canceled mark from the post office. "It was sent special delivery, but no one actually signed for it or noticed who dropped it off."

"How much time can you get off?" His question was abrupt and caught her off guard.

"I don't know."

The weary tone of her voice and the fact that she didn't argue with him pierced Kane's anger. He tossed the offending papers onto the desk before pulling her into his arms. "Don't worry, Hannah. He won't hurt you—not while I'm here," he promised.

"I know, Kane." Wrapping her arms around his waist, she had allowed a few frightened tears to drip into the hollow of his neck. "I'm sorry I didn't tell you before."

He refused to leave Hannah alone in the classroom while he arranged for her to have an extended leave of absence until the end of the semester. By that time the trial should be over and, hopefully, Sanchez would be in jail. Then she could resume her old life. A life in which he had no part.

Like some gallant knight of old, he had set his fate

on the path of justice. He couldn't ever remember a time when he hadn't wanted to be in law enforcement. Oh, sure, every kid wants to be a cop—right before they want to be an astronaut or a doctor. But his desire had never faltered. Immediately after high school he started taking courses in law enforcement and criminal justice at the local college. The day he turned twenty-one, he applied for acceptance to the police academy. Three months later he felt ten feet tall and bullet proof, ready to take on the world.

That feeling carried him through the first twenty minutes of his first actual day on the job. His Field Training Officer offered him two vital pieces of information: "Always tip the waitress in the coffee shop, and forget everything you learned in the academy."

Within a few months he found he possessed a natural talent for undercover work. Maybe it was his looks or just the fact that he didn't mind getting dirty and not shaving. But it seemed almost too simple for him to infiltrate the local drug scene. The Drug Enforcement Agency seemed a logical progression, and at twenty-four he had a new boss and way of life.

Until recently that way of life had suited him just fine. Lately, though, his thoughts had been centered around Hannah and the prospect of waking up with her each morning. Although he knew it was an impossibility, each day she managed to weave herself tighter into his thought processes.

Leaving Hannah's car in the school parking lot, Kane drove the old pickup truck he had hot-wired that morning toward the local convenience store and the nearest phone.

Cradling the phone with his shoulder, he punched in Eli's number. "Yeah, I need to speak with Eli."

"And whom may I say is calling?" The ultraprofessional voice on the other end asked.

"Uh . . . uh." In all of their concocting, they had forgotten to give him an alias. "I'm an old friend of his. I'm working out at Hannah McCord's."

"And your name, sir?" came the cool reply.

Who was she, the Dragon Lady Dispatcher? He had a vision of a six-foot-tall Amazon with a pistol strapped to her side and tobacco stuffed into her cheek. "Kane Leathers." He gave his new alias and hoped Eli would recognize his voice.

"Kane?" Eli's puzzled voice came on almost immediately.

"Yeah. Just wanted to let you know Ms. McCord has decided to take a leave of absence." He hoped the lawman was sharp enough to realize something was wrong.

"I'm sure the school will miss her," Eli offered quietly. "Does she need anything?"

"She wanted me to invite you out for supper tonight."

"Tell her I'll be out there at the usual time. I need to talk to her about an old friend of ours, anyway. I've been trying to track him down, but I'm not having any luck. It's as if he disappeared off the face of the earth." Eli broke the connection and Kane realized the lawman knew his business. It didn't take a genius to realize that the "old friend" Eli was talking about was Sanchez. The drug dealer had enough connections to disappear completely, but Kane had a suspicion he was only invisible to the law.

Roberto Sanchez had managed to build a small-time operation into one of the most powerful drug connections between Miami and L.A. When the task force

Seth was working with got a little too close, Sanchez had killed him without blinking an eye. If it hadn't been for A.L. Hardaway, Kane would probably be the one on trial—for Sanchez's murder.

After learning of his brother's death, Kane had been a man possessed. His very reason for living was to kill Sanchez. Luckily, A.L. kept him drunk long enough for the Albuquerque police to catch the drug lord and put him in jail to await trial. At the time Kane hadn't been very grateful. But eighteen months was long enough to gather a little perspective.

He'd give the courts their chance to put Sanchez away for good. But if Hannah got hurt, it would take more than friendship and a bottle of tequila to keep Kane from exacting his own revenge. He would take Sanchez apart a piece at a time and to hell with the consequences. A part of his soul had died with Seth. Without Hannah there would be nothing left.

"It's done, Mr. Sanchez," Tony said, holding the receiver close to his lips. There were too many people walking past the phone booth for him to give too many details.

"Excellent. I knew I could depend on you."

"I'll be waiting." Tony heard the click of the receiver and hung up. He didn't think his boss would really tell him to kill her just yet, but he had to be ready. Just before heading into the diner for lunch he wondered if he had made a mistake by not telling Sanchez about the man. The sheriff worried him, but not like the boyfriend. The blue-eyed stranger was not one he would like to meet in a dark alley. A smile curved his thin lips at the thought. Usually that's what people said about him.

SEVEN

Hannah barely had time to slip the catalogue under her music papers when Kane settled himself on the couch next to her. How on earth could she explain a catalogue full of sexy lingerie guaranteed to inflame even the most reluctant male? "What do you want?"

"Whoa, calm down." Although he was used to her snapping at him by now, he still didn't like it. "I just wondered what you were up to."

"I'm plotting to overthrow the government," she quipped. For three days she hadn't been able to turn around without running into either Kane or Eli. They must have worked out a shift schedule and it was driving her crazy. That, along with the fact that Kane seemed totally oblivious to her as a woman.

She tried everything she could think of to sweep him off his feet and into her bedroom—or his. Unfortunately, her knowledge of seduction techniques left a great deal to be desired. She batted her eyelashes, glossed her pouted lips, and dug out the pink angora sweater Seth had once thrown in the dryer.

The sweater almost worked. There had been a split second, as she sauntered into his bedroom to ask a completely inane question, when desire flickered in his eyes. Granted, it was only there briefly, but it gave her hope.

"How do you give a test in music?" he asked, grabbing a handful of graded papers.

An utterly wonderful scent wafted her way with his every movement and she sniffed gently in his direction. "What are you wearing?"

"Clothes," he answered, flipping through the papers. "Man, this Randy Matthews kid must be tone deaf."

"I meant your after-shave." She grabbed the paper from him and shuffled it into the pile on her lap, being extremely careful not to dislodge the catalogue. "Randy has a little trouble concentrating. That's all."

"How hard can it be?" He leaned closer, granting her another whiff.

"You'd be surprised," she answered. While she had never had a problem with daydreams before, she found herself lost in imagined ecstasy at least once or twice a day now. Never mind the nights! Closing her eyes to enjoy the aroma of clean male and unknown after-shave, she quickly conjured up another one of those erotic fantasies. It was foolish to be spending her time thinking about seducing Kane, when her life was in danger. *Was he pressing his thigh against hers on purpose?*

"Have you talked to his parents?" Kane asked in all innocence, never realizing he had just handed Hannah the answer to her dilemma.

"Dolly!" She sat up a little too quickly, sending the

papers sliding off her lap onto the floor. The catalogue made the journey last, falling open to a particularly exotic-looking woman semi-naked in a black teddy. Hannah felt her cheeks flame as Kane reached down to retrieve the glossy magazine.

Taking his time, he flipped through the pages, stopping occasionally to examine one of the outfits thoroughly. "Uh," he cleared his voice before turning the last page. "Were you planning to place an order?"

"Don't be ridiculous," she snapped, grabbing the book and piling papers on top of it. "It's junk mail. I was using it as a brace for my papers."

Kane didn't speak for a minute, and when he did, Hannah gave careful consideration to sewing his lips shut. "Don't bother, Hannah."

She waited until she heard the back door close before giving in to the temper tantrum that had been building since Kane arrived and began dictating her life. Unfortunately, after all the paper tossing and foot stomping were over, she was still in the same predicament. Hopelessly in love with a man who had never returned her feelings.

"Why?" she asked her reflection in the sparkling glass of the china cabinet. *Why?* Boy, was that the sixty-four-thousand-dollar question. *Why* had she fallen in love with Kane twelve years ago? *Why* was she still in love with him? And most importantly, *why* couldn't he feel the same way?

Oh, she knew all of his arguments. His job, the difference in their lifestyles, Seth. Mainly Seth. Twelve years ago she, too, had pushed aside her feelings for Kane out of loyalty to Seth. She worked hard at building a good life with her husband and had succeeded, too, for the most part.

Seth never even suspected her attraction to his brother. Hannah had done a good job of covering any occasional longings for what could never be, by throwing herself headlong into her marriage. And she could honestly say that never once had she pictured Kane while making love with Seth—not that he hadn't shown up once or twice during a particularly lurid dream. But Seth never knew—of that she was certain.

And if Seth were alive today, he still wouldn't know. While their marriage wasn't perfect, it wasn't the kind to be thrown away, either. Had a bullet not ended his life, she and Seth would have gone on together—comfortably, if not passionately, in love.

Well, comfortable had been nice. Now Hannah was ready for a little passion. If Sanchez should happen to be successful, she wanted to die knowing what it felt like to be swept away by her feelings. Even if it was just once. She was determined to know Kane McCord in every sense of the word. Picking up Randy Matthews' papers, she knew where to go for her answers.

Dolly Matthews had always been Hanson's "bad girl." Hannah could recall the hateful whispers of the other girls when Dolly sauntered down the hall in high school. Jealousy and ignorance had given the buxom redhead a reputation, whether she deserved it or not. Hannah questioned Eli about Dolly a time or two, but he always blushed and told her to stay away from Dolly.

Hannah could remember when Dolly packed her bags and left within thirty minutes of high school graduation. Not that most of the kids blamed her. At seventeen they were all itching to break free of the confines of small-town living.

In fact, some of them actually expressed admiration

for her courage at leaving behind all that they had grown to hate. Never being able to break any of the rules without your parents finding out about it before you got home; having to wait weeks before the hit movies were shown at the local drive-in; driving into the next county to buy beer; sitting down at five-thirty every day to watch the evening news and yearning to be a part of the real world.

Dolly had been a part of that real world, at least for a little while. When Gabriel Burnson's emphysema had forced him to retire, Dolly had come home to care for her father. Returning to Hanson last year with two young boys in tow, she had a worldly air that in no way improved her past reputation. Jealousy and ignorance still caused the hateful whispers.

Hannah didn't know if the rumors about her children being born out of wedlock were true and she really didn't care. In the few years she lived in Albuquerque as a cop's wife, she learned that nothing was ever quite as it seemed. There was no such thing as black and white, and the thin line between innocence and guilt was often blurred by the harsh realities of survival. Besides, who was Hannah to judge?

Without giving herself time to assess the intelligence of her plan, she picked up the phone and dialed Burnson's General Store. "Dolly, this is Hannah . . . Hanson McCord." If she didn't use her maiden name along with her married name, no one in town knew who she was. "I'm Randy's music teacher," she added for clarity.

"I know who you are, Hannah," came the whiskey-voiced reply. "What can I do for you?"

"I hate to bother you on Thanksgiving, but it's about Randy, his grades." Twirling the phone cord around her finger, she hurried on. "I'd like to talk to you if you're free."

"Do you want me to come to the school next week?" Dolly offered.

"I've taken a leave of absence for the rest of the semester, but I'm trying to get out report cards for this six weeks before I leave. I know how busy you are during the day," Hannah knew their conversation didn't belong in the utilitarian surroundings of Hanson Consolidated Schools. "How about tomorrow night?"

"Nope, my Friday nights aren't quite what they used to be." Dolly's rueful laugh easily conveyed her pain.

"Dolly . . ." What could she say? That she was sorry for what Dolly had suffered in the past? There were no words to replace the painful memories.

"Don't worry about it, Hannah." The reply was once again strong and capable. "Where should we meet?"

"I can come to your house." She hoped. Getting away from her two trained watch dogs was becoming almost impossible.

"Fine, Randy and Ricky will be over at Granny's for the holiday. Dad's medicine usually kicks in by eight."

"I'll be there around eight-thirty." Hannah found herself suddenly looking forward to seeing Dolly. While they had never been friends in the past, they hadn't been enemies, either. Hannah could use a friend. And she suspected Dolly could, too. "Can I bring anything?"

"Bring a six-pack if you've got one," Dolly chuckled after a brief pause.

"Done," Hannah promised, thinking of Kane's

brand-new cases of beer resting in her basement. "See ya then."

Breaking the connection, Hannah quickly cleaned up the remnants of her tantrum and began plotting. There had to be a way to slip away from Kane. He was pretty clever but no man was a match for a desperate woman with a mission.

Throwing back her shoulders, she decided to vent her frustration in the kitchen. It was nice cooking for a man again. Eli had a tendency to take her meals for granted, but Kane truly seemed to relish everything she placed in front of him. "Maybe I ought to strip down and stretch out on the dining table."

"Did you say something?" Kane asked, stepping in the back door. His hair was slightly disheveled and her fingers curled with the need to smooth it into place.

"Uh," Hannah scrambled for an answer, praying he hadn't overheard her comment. "I said I thought I would set the dining-room table tonight."

"What's wrong with the kitchen table?" Kane settled himself into one of the heavy oak chairs surrounding the table and tugged off his work boots. He had spent the last few days fixing things Hannah hadn't even known were broken. "There's no need to go to any trouble."

"I just thought it would be nice for Thanksgiving, but I won't if you don't want me to." Hannah wasn't about to argue over something she had no intention of doing in the first place. Watching as he lined his boots up next to hers in the pantry, she had a painfully domestic vision. "Go wash up."

"Yes, Mother." Kane offered a mock bow and sauntered out of the room with the ease of a man long accustomed to doing exactly as he pleased.

Frankly, Hannah was surprised at how well he was adjusting to . . . what? They weren't exactly living together, even though they shared everything but a bed. Cohabitating sounded much too modern for the feelings Hannah was experiencing. Her pangs of love and longing were as old as time.

"Did you use soap this time?" Hannah teased as Kane returned and opened the refrigerator for a beer. The tail of his unbuttoned shirt hung over the back of his jeans and his hair was damp. "Don't spoil your dinner."

"How do you suppose I managed to survive all these years without you to remind me what to do?" Kane's sarcasm was good-humored. Twisting the cap on the bottle, he made his way to lean against the counter beside her.

"I don't have any idea," she played along, slapping his hand as he reached into the salad bowl for a large slice of avocado. "Stop that."

"Stop what?" he asked, snatching a chunk of cheese from her fingers. "This?"

"Kane," she warned, brandishing her paring knife in his direction. "Do you want to eat?"

"I *am* eating," he argued, placing his hands on the counter, trapping her. With a low growl, he lowered his head and nibbled on the exposed skin of her neck.

The harsh ringing of the phone interrupted her musings and, extracting herself from his trap, she wiped her hands on a cup towel before answering it. "Hello?"

"There was a little girl who had a little curl right in the middle of her forehead. When she was good she was very very good, but when she talked she was so dead."

Hannah held the receiver away from her ear and

stared at it as if she expected to see someone. "Excuse me?"

A muted click, followed by the nagging buzz of the dial tone, was her only answer.

Fear, quick and breathtaking in its intensity, swept up her spine as she slammed the receiver down and turned to stare at the back door. Years ago she wouldn't have been concerned about the caller being close by. Now, with the invention of portable cellular phones, she knew it was possible the man was standing on her back porch. "Kane!"

"I know, I know. Stay out of the salad," came the disgruntled reply.

"Forget the damned salad." Hannah pressed her back against the wall and fought against the hysteria running through her mind.

"What the hell is going on?" Kane took one look at the fear in Hannah's eyes and pulled her into his embrace. "Is it Diogee?"

Wrapping her arms around his waist, Hannah shivered slightly before telling him about the call. "Do you think it was Sanchez?"

"That son of a —" Kane tightened his hold on her for a second before taking her face in his hands. Turning her lips to his, he gave her a gentle kiss before releasing her. "Are you sure that's all he said?"

"Yes." Hannah nodded and turned to stare out the kitchen window.

"Can you remember anything else?" Kane asked. "Did it sound like long distance? Was there any background noise?"

"It might have been long distance," Hannah admitted, relaxing slightly with the idea. "His voice did sound odd. Sort of like he was in a barrel."

"Probably a cordless phone," Kane surmised and picked up the phone. "I better call Eli."

"He's probably already on his way here," she commented, glancing at the clock on the stove. "I told him we would eat around five."

Hanging up, Kane pulled Hannah close to him and led her into the family room. "Will you let me call someone and have a safe house set up?"

"No." She shook her head. "I don't like the idea of my life depending on strangers."

"Hannah . . ." he began, but stopped at the look on her face.

"Please," she pleaded softly, her hand tightening in his. "Surely you and Eli can handle it."

"Okay, this time. But if there are any more threats, you're going to a safe house." He pulled her onto his lap. Eli found them in that position when he arrived a few minutes later.

"Excuse me, but I was expected, wasn't I?" A slight reddish tint flushed his cheeks as he strolled into the room and tossed his hat onto the coffee table.

"Of course." Hannah swiped at her eyes, not wanting Eli to see just how frightened she really was. "We were just waiting for you."

"Yeah, right." Eli didn't bother to hide his playful sarcasm.

"I'll have dinner on the table in a few minutes," she promised. "Eli, would you like a beer?"

"Hey," Kane protested. "I thought it would spoil our dinner?"

"Eli works for a living," Hannah argued as if it made perfect sense. Actually she just needed to be out of the room for a few minutes to gather the scattered remnants of her courage and tie them back together.

She knew Kane would apprise Eli of the situation and the men would spend the entire evening plotting a new strategy for her protection. Intellectually, she knew it was a good idea, but emotionally she still had a hard time dealing with the fact that her life might be in danger.

She understood the risks, really she did. She couldn't seem to make Kane and Eli believe that she had no intention of acting foolish. Hadn't she agreed to let Kane drive her to town whenever she needed to buy something? Didn't she dutifully check in with Eli every half hour? Wasn't she giving up *everything* in her life for the next two and a half weeks? Not that breaking a date with Gordie Simmons was a major sacrifice, it was simply the unfairness of it all.

Here she sat, terrified in her own home while Sanchez was running around free. *He* could go out to dinner with friends. *He* could walk down the street without jumping at every shadow. *He* could sleep in his bed at night and not worry about having his throat slit. Her anger at the fact that Sanchez could enjoy this freedom was the only thing that kept her from giving in to her fears.

She used her rage now to fight back the horrible reality of her life and look forward. The trial was only two weeks away and then the nightmare would be over. In the meantime, she would spend her energy trying to convince Kane that she wasn't only Seth's widow. Hopefully, with Dolly's help, she would be able to show him just how very much she needed him—not as a frightened witness but as a friend, a woman, and a lover.

EIGHT

"Okay, honey, you had the chicken-fried steak with extra gravy and a cup of coffee, right?" The waitress placed a large platter of food in front of Kane. "You need ketchup for those fries?"

"Where would I put it?" Kane asked. The heavily battered fried steak took up over half his plate. A rich white gravy not only covered the meat but most of his french fries and green beans as well. "Is this a joke?"

"What?" Wanda glanced down at the plate.

"Do they always serve this much food or am I special?"

Cocking her head to the side, she surveyed him for a second. "Well, you look pretty special, but Mamie always dishes out gobs of food. People around here like to get their money's worth."

After several bites, Kane decided the good folks of Hanson had no idea what a treasure they had in Mamie Turnbow. This was absolutely the best chicken-fried steak he had ever tasted. The hot rolls were probably the closest thing to ambrosia this side of Mount Olympus, and when Wanda placed a giant slice of lemon meringue pie in front of him, he actually groaned his pleasure.

A glance at his watch told him he still had half an hour before picking up Hannah from her parent-teacher conference with Dolly Matthews. He had reluctantly agreed to allow Hannah time alone with the woman, but only because Dolly's house was situated right next door to the diner. She hadn't even complained when he wanted to check out the alley before dropping her off.

"What else can I get you?" Wanda asked, placing his ticket face down on the speckled linoleum tabletop. "Another piece of pie?"

"Just coffee." Kane watched as she filled the ancient mug to the brim.

"You that fellow living with Hannah?"

"Yep, that's me." Kane already suspected everyone in the diner knew exactly who he was, but Wanda was the first one who actually broached the subject.

"I'm Wanda Turnbow, Mamie's daughter-in-law." She held out her hand and gave his a firm shake. "We sure think the world of Hannah around here."

"I'm glad to hear that," he said. "I do, too."

"Yeah?" Wanda's smile didn't quite reach her eyes. "Then why aren't you marryin' her instead of just shackin' up?"

Caught off guard by the question, Kane merely shrugged his shoulders. "I guess you better ask Hannah?"

"Guess I will," Wanda assured and sauntered away to divulge the new information she had just obtained. Within minutes everyone in the room was speculating about Hannah's relationship with the blue-eyed man in the front booth.

Next door, Hannah was wondering about the same thing. It hadn't taken Dolly long to figure out that Hannah had an ulterior motive for their meeting. Once pressed, Hannah confessed.

"I need help," she admitted, accepting Dolly's offer of a drink. "It has to do with a man."

"Lord, honey, anytime a woman needs help you can bet a man is involved." Dolly used the edge of a butter knife to pop the top on her can. "Is it Eli or that hunk of dynamite that dropped you off?"

"Eli?" Hannah almost choked on a mouthful of beer. "Why on earth would you think this was about Eli?"

Dolly grabbed a handful of potato chips before answering. "Everybody in town figures it's just a matter of time before you two tie the knot."

"That's ridiculous," Hannah protested. "We're only friends."

"Sometimes that's better than being lovers." Dolly didn't bother to hide the pain in her voice.

"And sometimes it's not." Hannah's voice held her own sorrow and the two women realized they might have something in common after all.

"Okay, what can I do?"

Grateful that Dolly was actually offering to help, Hannah explained about Kane's reluctance to become involved. "I know he's attracted to me but how do I get him to . . ."

"To take you to bed?" Dolly finished.

Blushing, Hannah nodded. "It's not just that. I mean, I could find a man to have sex with, but I want more. I want . . . Heck, I'm not exactly sure what I want.''

"I know," Dolly whispered. Raising her eyes to Hannah's, she continued. "You want the kind of passion that's only possible when two people really love and respect each other."

"Yeah," Hannah agreed quickly. "That's exactly what I want. Now, how do I get it?"

"Beats the heck out of me." Dolly watched Hannah sip her beer for a minute. "Listen, Hannah, if I knew how to do that, do you think I would be sitting here in Hanson taking care of two kids alone?"

"I guess I just thought . . ." Hannah paused, searching for the right phrase. "I mean you always had a date on Friday night."

"Yeah, I always had a date all right." Dolly stared out the window as if she could see herself as she had been all those years ago. "What you don't realize is that most of the time I only got those dates because the guy thought I was a sure thing. You have no idea of how many times I was dumped out at the curb because I wouldn't 'put out'."

"How awful." Hannah couldn't ever remember a boy pushing her beyond the boundaries of decency. Never once had a date not picked her up at the front door, met her parents, and kissed her politely under the yellow porch light when he brought her home. On time.

"Yeah, well, don't worry about it." Dolly's smile was firmly in place. "I survived. When Jack Matthews decided marriage to me wasn't what he had in mind, I got the fastest divorce I could and hightailed it home. Look, I may not have found Mr. Right the first time, but I've got two terrific kids to show for my marriage. Even if Randy *can't* carry a tune in a bucket."

Bolstered by Dolly's show of bravado, Hannah forged on. "I know this relationship may not stand a snowball's chance in hell, but I've got to try. This man has been haunting my dreams for the last twelve years. Now I've got him safely tucked away in my spare bedroom. There has to be a way to get him across the hall."

"With that kind of determination, I'd say the man doesn't stand a chance." Dolly held her beer can aloft and toasted Kane's defeat. "Watch out, Kane Leathers, you are about to meet your match."

It didn't take the two women long to concoct a plan. By the time Hannah had polished off her third beer, the seduction of Kane McCord "Leathers" was in full swing.

"Should I buy a Frank Sinatra tape?" Hannah giggled.

"Why not?" Dolly lowered her voice and hummed an old familiar tune.

"Okay." Hannah grabbed another beer out of Dolly's refrigerator and went over their plan. "Dim lights, shoft music, and a sexy dress." Frowning, Hannah glanced down at her bright-orange sweater and blue jeans. "The only problem I shee is with my wardrobe."

"What's wrong with it?" Dolly picked up on Hannah's slurred words and quietly replaced her beer with a soda.

"Shee these jeans?" Hannah slapped her hands on her rear for emphasis. "Thish is all I own. Thish and teacher clothes."

"What about your lingerie?" Pressing a bowl of pretzels at Hannah, Dolly grinned at her inebriated friend's look of dismay.

"I only have two nightgowns," Hannah muttered in

disgust. "And both of them are cutesy white cotton things. I want sumthin' bold and daring." With an exaggerated swivel of her hips, Hannah strutted down the hall to Dolly's bedroom.

Settling a slightly weaving Hannah onto the edge of her bed, Dolly knelt and pulled a storage box out of the bottom of her closet. "I've got a few things in here from my bridal shower that might do the trick. I've never even worn them. I mean when you're marrying an English professor you don't exactly parade around in red bustiers and fish net stockings."

"You married an English processor?" Hannah tried to focus on Dolly. "I didn't know that."

"Most people don't," Dolly assured, holding up a bright-peach teddy trimmed with rows of lace. "Can you imagine giving someone with this hair an orange teddy? It would be perfect with your coloring, though."

Grabbing the wispy bit of cloth, Hannah held it up to her chest. "I won't fill it out—you know, on top."

"I don't think it'll be a problem," Dolly consoled before handing her a black see-through nightgown with matching robe. "This is very elegant, just like you."

"Thanks." Tears filled Hannah's eyes and she couldn't imagine why. Of course, she couldn't figure out why the end of her nose was numb, either. "Thish is bootiful."

"Someone's at the door," Dolly said, rising from her position on the floor. "You wait right here."

"Okay." Hannah reached down to feel the silky material of the nightgown. "Would you like this, Kane?"

Dolly wasn't surprised to find the object of Hannah's fascination standing on her front porch. "Come on in."

"Is Hannah ready?" he asked, his eyes glancing around the living room.

"She's in the back of the house," Dolly told him. "We're sorting through some things. Can you come back in about an hour?"

"We really need to be heading back to the house." Kane didn't like the look in Dolly's eyes. She was hiding something. "If you'll just call Hannah."

"I don't think she's ready to leave yet," Dolly persisted.

"Help!" Hannah's muffled wail put an end to the debate.

"What the hell?" Kane pushed past a startled Dolly and ran in the direction of Hannah's voice. "Hannah!"

"In here."

A frisson of fear sliced through him at the panic in her voice and he thrust open the bedroom door. Stopping dead in his tracks, he examined the scene before him. "What in the hell do you think you are doing?"

"I'm trapped," Hannah mumbled through layers of sheer black nylon. "I can't move."

Kane knew exactly how she felt. From his vantage point in the doorway, he was witness to the most perfect vision he could ever hope to see. Swathed from head to toe in a black nightgown, a naked Hannah was struggling to remove her head from the armhole. Her left arm along with one perky breast was completely exposed by what he supposed was a plunging neckline and her backside was plainly visible through the sheer material. He glanced from Hannah to the king-size bed and groaned. "What is wrong with you?"

"I'm being hanged by linguini."

"Linguini?" He had seen plenty of underwear in his time but he hadn't ever heard of any made from pasta. "Don't you mean lingerie?"

"Don't shtand there like a blimp on a log," she cried. "Get me out of this."

"Hannah!" Dolly gasped, as she hurried into the room. "Good grief, girl, what a mess."

"How am I ever gonna deduce him if I can't get thish thing on?" With Dolly's help Hannah managed to find the neck of the gown. "There. Don't you think he'll like this?"

"Yes, Hannah," Dolly agreed, quickly wrapping the matching robe around Hannah's shoulders. "Let's get you out of this and back into your clothes."

"Nope." Hannah shook her head and hugged the robe to her. "I'll never be able to get it on again."

"Hannah," Dolly cajoled. "You can't ride home in this."

"Yes I can."

"Would you help me?" Dolly asked Kane. "Quit laughing at her and help me get her clothes on."

"She's drunk."

"No kidding," Dolly dead-panned. "Gee, you must be a whiz at party games. Now are you gonna help me or not?"

"Come here, Hannah," Kane ordered, grabbing her discarded blue jeans.

"No!" She stomped her foot and wrapped the robe tighter.

Tired of playing the game, he merely shrugged and stalked across the room. "Have it your way."

"What are you doing?" Dolly squealed as Kane lifted Hannah over his shoulder and turned toward the door.

"Taking her home to sleep this off." Without another word Kane marched through the house and out the door.

Dolly stood on the front porch watching Kane gently settle a still-jabbering Hannah into the pickup. "I ought to be asking her for pointers."

Kane glanced over at Hannah as she chatted about several things that made absolutely no sense at all. As miffed as he was by her condition, he couldn't keep from grinning at her painfully honest confessions. She would hate herself in the morning—if she remembered. "Hannah, baby, why don't you take a nap until we get home."

"But I'm not a bit sheepy," she assured before dutifully leaning her head on his shoulder and closing her eyes. Within seconds she was asleep.

"What am I gonna do with you, Hannah Elizabeth McCord?" he asked, before placing a gentle kiss on top of her head.

Keeping his eyes on the road, he purposely ignored her erotically clad form. Although he had witnessed the perfection of her body on other occasions, tonight was different. Tonight she had been dressing for a man. Drunk or not, Hannah had donned the nightgown with one purpose in mind, seduction.

She didn't really understand what she was doing, he argued to himself. It was only her situation. He represented justice—security. Hannah couldn't possibly want him. He was just a link to Seth. A substitute for his brother.

No, dammit. He wouldn't give in to his need for Hannah. He had refused to challenge his brother for her all those years ago and he wouldn't compete with his memory now. Until he was positive Hannah wanted him for who he was, Kane McCord, he wouldn't touch her. Even if it meant cutting off both his hands.

"Kane?" Hannah roused as he brought the pickup to a stop in front of the house.

"Shh," he whispered, lifting her into his arms. "We're home."

" 'Kay," she murmured against his neck and Kane automatically began reciting multiplication tables. It worked for Jethro on the *Beverly Hillbillies*, why not him.

It took some maneuvering, but he managed to unlock the door without putting her down. His arms ached by the time he laid her on her quilt-covered bed. "Go to sleep, Hannah."

Nodding slightly, Hannah shifted so he could pull the quilt over her, removing temptation from his sight. "Come to bed."

Gritting his teeth, Kane slowly backed from the room. *Come to bed.* In her alcohol-fogged mind she must have been talking to Seth.

"Of course she was talking to Seth, you idiot," he chastised himself before sliding between the cold empty sheets across the hall. "It couldn't possibly be you she wants in her bed."

Hannah squinted against the bright glare of sunlight streaming through her bedroom window and groaned. Her head felt as if she had slept on rollers and her mouth was as dry as a Panhandle summer. A low rumble from the pit of her stomach reminded her of last night's folly.

So this was a hangover. She had heard about them before, but since she rarely drank more than an occasional wine cooler, this was her first. "Hannah, you idiot."

She had a vague recollection of being attacked by

Dolly's nightgown, but other than that, she was blank. "Some woman of the world you are, Hannah McCord. I'll bet Kane was really swept away by your feminine wiles."

Mortified by what he must think of her, she rolled over and pulled the covers above her head. "Ouch," she cried as something dug into the delicate flesh of her cheek.

Rising up slightly, she glanced down at the bloodred rose lying on the white muslin pillowcase. The thought of who must have been responsible for the gift chased away any traces of a hangover. "Kane."

Grimacing at the bitter taste in her mouth, Hannah hurried to the bathroom to brush her teeth and spray just a tad of perfume behind her knees. Still swathed in Dolly's peignoir, she paused outside his door to consider her actions.

Did the rose mean what she thought—hoped—it did? Had Kane finally overcome his guilt at desiring his late brother's wife? Once she stepped over that threshold there would be no turning back. Dressed as she was, there could be no doubt as to what was on her mind.

Would he offer her a groggy smile before flipping back the edge of the quilt for her to join him? Or would he yawn and tell her he wanted pancakes for breakfast? There was only one way to find out.

"I guess this is what they mean by screwing your courage to the sticking place," she whispered, as her hand grasped the antique crystal doorknob. The door swung open without a sound and she took a minute to release the breath she had been holding.

Good grief, the man was even sexy when he was asleep. His dark hair was a vivid contrast against the sunshine white of his pillowcase and she almost reached out to brush an errant curl off his face. The soft wedding ring quilt molded itself to the hard contours of his body as he sprawled across the entire width of the double bed.

She had given consideration to simply sliding into the warm cocoon of his slumber, but his bed-hogging ruined that plan. It would have been so much simpler to be in his arms when he awakened.

"What do you want?" Kane asked without ever opening his eyes or changing the rhythm of his breathing.

She should have known she would never be able to sneak up on him. Sitting on the edge of the bed, she gently placed her hand on his cheek. "I just wanted to thank you."

"No need," he replied, thinking she was referring to last night. He had hoped she wouldn't be too embarrassed by her actions, but he hadn't expected her to be this calm. "Don't worry about it."

"I'm not worried about it," she assured him, holding the rose up to sniff its gentle fragrance.

"Fine." Peering through the thick fringe of his eyelashes, he watched her brush the velvety petals across her equally soft lips and was immediately aroused. Tugging the quilt around his neck, he wondered if she knew how beautiful she was.

Without warning, Hannah stood up and allowed the concealing robe to drop to the floor before sliding her slender frame beneath the quilt. "I hope I didn't misunderstand."

Any opportunity for a graceful retreat was abruptly ended as her smooth, naked legs entwined with his muscular ones. Desire filled her eyes, but her voice was laced with uncertainty as she snuggled closer. "I didn't, did I?"

She wanted him! His mind rang with the realization. In the clear light of day, without any alcohol clouding her judgment, Hannah Elizabeth Hanson McCord wanted *him*. "Are you sure, babe?"

"Oh, yes, Kane." Tilting her face, she anticipated his kiss. It wasn't a long wait.

He pulled her flush against his chest before taking her mouth—hot and hard. His mouth suckled hers as his tongue begged for entry. Nipping his bottom lip with her small white teeth, she opened her mouth for him.

With shaking fingers, he plucked at the silky material of her gown before managing to slide it off her shoulders, exposing the delicate flesh of her throat to his searching lips. Lower and lower he delved, seeking the treasures of her body. Catching her gown in his teeth, he ripped the material until he revealed the fragile perfection of her breast.

His breath caught as his eyes feasted on the woman in his arms. Delighting in her soft angles and gentle curves, he proceeded to tell her of his admiration. He praised every inch of her body with his lips and tongue as he worked her gown down the length of her body. "So beautiful, so perfect."

"I agree," she whispered, caressing the hard contours of his chest and stomach before pulling him up to lie beside her. "Love me, Kane. Now."

"We have all day, Hannah. I intend to love every sweet inch of you before you leave my bed," he promised, and stripped off his own briefs. Placing her hand on his chest, he whispered against her ear. "I believe you were doing some exploring of your own."

"I'm not very good at this, Kane," she admitted, blushing at what he must think of her. "You might need to help me."

"I'm sure you'll do just fine, honey." His hand captured hers and brought it to his lips. Turning her palm to his mouth, he traced a path with his tongue. "That's your love line."

"What does it say?"

"It says you are a very passionate woman," he grinned before capturing her other hand and repeating the process. "It says that you have ways of turning mere mortal men into slaves."

"Hmm." She held up her palm to examine the line he had traced. "And to think I might never have known."

"I'm glad I could teach you." His words held a meaning they both understood. Although he knew she and Seth must have made love hundreds of times, it was important for this time—their first time—to be special.

"I am, too."

Deciding he had better things to do than discuss palmistry, Kane resumed his quest. He took great care seeking and finding those things that would give Hannah the most pleasure as she lay in his arms. He reveled in the honest emotions she revealed to him as his fingers explored her desire. She didn't bite her tongue to keep from crying out as his lips brushed across the tips of her breasts and she didn't try to hide her body's reaction to his manipulations.

Neither was she a passive partner. She was an equal participant in their journey, striving to give him the same pleasure he was wringing from her love-starved body. Time after time she would open herself to him, but he would merely take a sample before continuing to tease and torment until her body was aching for fulfillment.

"Please," she begged, her breath shallow with longing.

"Who am I?" he asked, poised above her, his legs sliding down between hers.

"Kane," she whispered. Then again—louder. "Kane."

Slipping inside her, he remained motionless as he brushed kisses across her cheeks and down her throat. "You belong to me now, Hannah. You're mine." The words were torn from him, as if he hadn't meant to share them with her.

"Always," she agreed, urging him to move. "I love you."

Their exploring had taken its toll on their restraint and within minutes they were crying out their satisfaction. Burying her face in the crook of his neck, Hannah shuddered with her release. "Thank you."

"Don't thank me, Hannah," he protested, rolling onto his back and cradling her to his side. "We did this with each other—for each other. It's the most special moment of my life."

Shocked by this blatant admission, Hannah reached over to retrieve the rose from the nightstand. "I never would have had the nerve to come to you, if not for this."

"A rose?"

"When I found it on my pillow this morning, I knew you cared." She held up the rose to caress the rough texture of his jaw. "Was I wrong?"

"Hannah . . ." Kane's voice was suddenly harsh as he grabbed the rose from her fingers. Crushing the petals, he flung the flower to the bed. "I didn't leave this damn rose on your pillow."

"Of course you did." Sitting up as he vaulted out of bed, she watched him pull on his clothes. In the space of a heartbeat her lover was gone, replaced by a reality-hardened man intent on his job. "Kane?"

Turning to face her as he struggled with the zipper of his jeans, he shook his head. "I wish I could tell you I did."

Staring at the petals scattered among the tangled sheets, Hannah shivered with the harsh reality of what he was telling her. "Sanchez did it. He came into my house and put that rose on my pillow." Tears brimmed in her eyes and she allowed them to fall unchecked. "You must think I'm a fool."

In two strides Kane was across the room pulling Hannah into his arms. "I don't think you're a fool. Regardless of what brought you to me this morning, I wanted you. Never doubt that, Hannah."

Swiping at her tears, she allowed anger to replace her humiliation. "Okay, what do we do now? About Sanchez, I mean."

"The first thing you do is pack a bag and then we get the hell out of here." Kane grabbed his duffle bag and filled it with what few items of clothing he possessed. "I'll call Eli and let him know we're coming."

"It'll only take me a second." Tugging the sheet loose from the foot of the bed, Hannah wrapped it around her as she scurried across the hallway. With the horrifying reminder of Sanchez and his threats, she felt like an endangered species.

From the relatively safe confines of her bedroom, she heard Kane talking on the phone. Assuming he was apprising Eli of the situation, she quickly began filling a suitcase with those things she deemed appropriate for her situation.

What did one pack for running? She couldn't recall ever reading a section in one of the fashion magazines outlining the proper attire for fleeing a known criminal. Jogging shoes and a camouflage hat, she supposed.

"You ready?" Kane called from the hallway.

"What should I take?"

Stepping into the room, he surveyed the mass of clothing she had considered and discarded. "Jeans and sweaters. Underwear and something to sleep in. Good walking shoes or boots. This isn't a beauty contest, Hannah." Not bothering to wait for her reply, Kane spun on his heel and headed down the stairs.

"I know that." Shoving another pair of jeans into her overnight bag, she grabbed one of her white baby-doll pajamas and frowned. She just couldn't see Kane ripping that off with his teeth. The memory of his ardor caused a satisfied grin to replace her scowl. Kane hadn't rejected her love, and although he hadn't said it, she suspected his feelings for her were just as deep.

"Hannah!"

Grabbing her suitcase, Hannah's gaze swept across the room that had been her sanctuary from the real world. The soft-ivory walls had listened as she cried out her pain. The window had allowed the sun and moon to remind her that life went on. The too-soft bed had been her oasis in the overwhelming vastness of her despair. Now it had been sullied, desecrated by Sanchez.

The man had taken almost every reason she had for living, but he hadn't defeated her yet. Seth would live on in the memory of those who had loved him and Diogee was getting stronger every day. Someday she would return to this room—safe and happy.

Until then she would do whatever it took to stay

alive. Sanchez might have stolen her freedom, but he had unknowingly given her a precious gift. He had given her Kane.

There might be a future for them after all, she mused. That is, if Sanchez didn't slip into her bedroom at night and slit her throat.

"You had no problems getting into the house?"

Tony thought of how ridiculously easy it had been to slip into the farmhouse and leave the rose on her pillow. "None. What's next?"

A brief pause. "We wait. So far the woman is still planning to testify. If we can't change her mind . . ." *Sanchez saw no need to finish the sentence. Both men knew precisely what would happen if Hannah didn't back down.*

NINE

"Would you slow down?" Hannah grabbed the door for support as the pickup bounced over a large pothole in the road. "I won't have to worry about Sanchez—you'll kill us before we get to town."

"The sooner I get you to Eli, the better." The muscles in Kane's forearms bunched as he strained to keep the rickety vehicle between the bar ditches. The ancient pickup didn't possess anything as modern as power steering and it was difficult to maneuver at a high speed.

Knowing he didn't really want to get rid of her, Hannah swallowed her retort to the stinging remark. Kane had berated himself for the last five minutes and she wished he would let up. "It's my fault."

"What is?" His eyes never left the road and he didn't reach over to touch her, but some of the hostility had left his voice.

"This whole thing." Staring out the side window of the truck, Hannah watched the pale sun-washed prairie whiz by. Only an occasional rise saved the land from being absolutely flat. Pastel fields of tan and yellow were dotted with cattle storing up for the winter that would surely arrive soon. "If I hadn't been drunk last night you would have noticed that someone had been in the house. I would have seen the rose when I went to bed."

"Would you stop making excuses for me?" His voice was infused with disgust. "I'm here to protect you. Nothing else."

Tears sprang to Hannah's eyes and she kept her face averted so he wouldn't notice how much his words hurt. *Nothing else.* Certainly not making love in the morning. Or the afternoon. Or at midnight. "I'm still alive."

Barely braking at the lone stoplight in the middle of town, Kane sped through the intersection on his way toward the sheriff's office. "No thanks to me. I'm sure the rose is only a warning."

"I thought he wanted me dead?" Hannah automatically raised her hand in greeting as they rushed past the grocery store. Wanda Turnbow waved back on her way in.

"He only wants to make sure you don't testify," Kane clarified. "He probably expects you to contact the D.A. and refuse to show up in Albuquerque. If you don't back down . . ." His pause was fraught with meaning but Kane felt compelled to spell it out for her. "He will kill you."

"I am testifying." Hannah sat straighter in the seat, facing him for the first time since leaving the farm. "If it *is* the *last* thing I ever do in this world, I'm sending that man to prison."

"Okay." He nodded, whipping the truck across the

road to pull up in front of the station. "Then we do this my way."

Without any warning, Kane grabbed her by the wrist and hauled her across the seat and onto the sidewalk. Pulling her along behind him, he pushed the door of the sheriff's office open with one hand while shoving her through the door with the other.

A petite woman behind the desk jumped to her feet as they barged through the door. Kane was surprised at her appearance. What happened to the Amazon from hell? This woman looked like a stiff wind would blow her away. With his right hand he dug his billfold out of his back pocket and thrust his badge into her face. "You must be Texetta. I need the sheriff and a cell."

"What?" Texetta glanced from Kane to Hannah, her mouth gaping open like a trout. "Hannah, what in the world is going on?"

"A cell?" Hannah tried to tug her wrist from Kane's grip. "What do you need a cell for?"

"You." Without waiting for any further questions from the confused women, Kane yanked Hannah behind him until he located the cells. Deciding the small holding cell directly behind Eli's office offered the greatest security, he propelled Hannah through the doors and slammed them shut.

Stalking toward a metal locker standing in the corner of Eli's office, he flung open the door to reveal a myriad of law-enforcement equipment. He was surprised to locate a flak jacket hanging inside. Grabbing the heavy black protective garment, he took it to Hannah. Shoving it through the bars, he ordered, "Put this on and stay away from the door."

"You have lost your mind." Hannah let the jacket fall to the floor with a thud. "Let me out of here."

"You agreed to doing this my way," he reminded her. "Now put on the damned jacket and get away from the door before I handcuff you to the toilet."

Reading the truth in his eyes, Hannah hefted the jacket to her shoulders and struggled under the weight of thirty-five pounds of material designed to save her life. "How long do I have to stay in here?"

"Until I let you out." With that he was gone, leaving her alone to ponder the strange events of the last several minutes.

Flopping down on the thin cot in the back corner of the cell, Hannah wrapped the too-large vest around her and pouted. The austere surroundings of the cell might be conducive to scaring the beegebers out of one of the local teenage boys, but Hannah couldn't appreciate that fact right now. She hated the sterile white cinderblock walls and hard concrete floor. The sight of the small sink and toilet in the opposite corner did nothing to bolster her spirits.

Where was Kane going? And where was Eli? "Texetta?"

"What is it, honey?" The small woman immediately appeared in the doorway.

"Let me out of here."

Shaking her head, Texetta glanced over her shoulder before whispering, "That man would kill me. You just sit tight until the sheriff gets here. He'll know what to do."

"Where is Eli?" Hannah knew she could probably cajole Texetta into letting her out, but she didn't want to face Kane's wrath.

"I don't know, but I've already paged him." Texetta glanced over her shoulder as if she expected Kane to swoop down on them. "He should have been in by now. He had a late call last night. Gabriel Burnson had some difficulty and that daughter of his called Eli about ten o'clock last night. I didn't come on duty till midnight, but he never did check back in."

"Okay." Hannah forced a smile she didn't know she had. "I just hope he hurries." With a shudder, Hannah surveyed her surroundings.

"Don't worry about the cell being clean, honey," Texetta assured her before leaving Hannah alone. "I had to scrub it out yesterday after Darren Wilcox was in for DWI. My heavens, you should have seen the mess that man made."

Knowing exactly what kind of mess Darren was capable of, Hannah cast a doubtful glance at the mattress she was resting on. "It's just not fair."

By the time Eli finally arrived, Hannah's nerves were stretched taut and she had built up a sweat under the heavy jacket. "Where have you been?" she yelled as he walked through the door to her cell. Struggling to get to her feet, she was grateful when her friend reached down and hauled her into his embrace.

"Sorry about this, Hannah," he ground out, squeezing her tightly.

Returning his hug, Hannah allowed him to support her weight. "Can I get out of here?"

"Sure, come on into my office until Kane gets back." Eli ushered her through the pristine white hall leading to his office and helped her into a chair. "Want some coffee?"

"I could use something," Hannah agreed, shrugging out of the jacket. "How do you wear that thing?"

"I don't usually," Eli commented, handing her a steaming cup of coffee. "What's going on here? Did someone take a shot at you?"

"Haven't you talked to Kane?" Hannah was puzzled by Eli's lack of knowledge. "I thought Kane called you from the house."

"Not as far as I know." A slight blush tinted his cheeks before he cleared his voice and continued. "I was out of the house this morning, so maybe he couldn't get ahold of me."

Hannah wondered at his reluctance to be more specific but didn't press. She had enough to handle without being worried about Eli's activities. Instead of pushing the issue of his whereabouts, she filled him in on what had transpired that morning. Well, not all of it.

She left out the fact that she had spent time in Kane's bed—in his arms—but she did explain about finding the rose. "I don't even know how he got in the house."

"Does Kane suspect it was Sanchez?"

"I don't really know what he thinks," she admitted. "He told me to pack a bag and then he threw me in jail. It would have to be Sanchez, though, wouldn't it?"

Eli shook his head, taking a sip of coffee. "I doubt it. He would send one of his soldiers to do the dirty work. He can't afford to handle this personally."

"How many men does he have?" Hannah glanced out the window in Eli's office to stare at the few people strolling down the street. She recognized almost every face, but now and then a stranger would appear. Was the man with the dark sunglasses and black shirt the one who had left the rose on her pillow? How about the blond surfer-looking guy walking into Mamie's Diner? Was he concealing a gun inside those wild, printed pants?

"Don't worry about it, Junebug." Eli came around his desk to rub her shoulders. "We'll take care of you.

I talked with that friend of Kane's at the DEA and there's a safe house already lined up for you. They really know what they're doing.''

''Which is more than I can say for you.'' Kane's voice startled them and they both spun in the direction of the door. ''What are you doing in here? And why aren't you wearing that vest?''

''Because it's too hot,'' she protested when he held it up for her to put on. ''No one is going to shoot me in Eli's office.''

''Put it on.'' The tone of his voice could have cut steel, and with a beseeching glance at Eli, Hannah slipped her arms into the heavy garment. ''I'll wear it, but I'm not going back into that cell.''

''Hannah!'' Kane warned, but this time Eli did step in.

''Look, this room is equipped with bulletproof glass and a steel door.'' He indicated the thick metal door Kane was leaning against. ''It's just as safe as the cell.''

''Why the glass?'' Kane asked. It wasn't usual for a small-town sheriff to doctor his office so heavily.

''Sheriff Turner got to be pretty paranoid before he was forced to retire. That's why I've got a flak jacket and all those other goodies in the locker.'' Eli nodded his head toward the cabinet Kane had plundered earlier. ''I always thought the old coot was crazier than a bed-bug for buying all this stuff, but it sure might come in handy now.''

''All right.'' Kane turned to Hannah. The jacket hung almost to her knees and the dark color only served to accentuate her pale features. She looked lost and frightened. The picture she made tugged at his heart but he forced himself to remember the rose and his

failure to protect her. As much as he wanted to wrap
her in his arms, he didn't dare. "You can stay in here
as long as the door is shut and you're with one of us."

"How long before you make your move?" Eli asked
briskly. The emotions were running high in his tiny
office and he was uncomfortable turning Hannah over
to anyone.

"A.L. already has a house, and backup should be
there within two hours." Kane checked his watch before continuing. "All we have to do is figure a way to
get her out of town without being followed."

"Where is the house?" Eli asked, turning to a large
New Mexico map pinned to his office wall.

"I can't tell you that," Kane started.

"Kane!" Hannah was appalled. "Eli would never
tell anyone. I trust him with my life." As if to offer
proof, Hannah walked across the office and wrapped
her arms around Eli.

"I understand," Eli assured Kane before returning
Hannah's awkward hug. "Don't worry, Junebug, he's
just doing his job."

"Well, if this isn't a fine how-do-you-do," a sultry
voice called from the doorway, sending Kane into a
defensive position. His hand was more than halfway to
his gun before he recognized Dolly.

"Dolly!" Eli jerked free of Hannah and faced the
woman whose arms he had just left. "This isn't what
it looks like."

Stunned speechless by the sight of a stammering,
blushing Eli, Hannah could only grin as her friend
rushed across the room toward the redhead. "We were
only—"

"Oh, hush up," Dolly ordered with a wave of her
hand. "I know there isn't anything between you two."

"You do?" Eli was confused by her lack of temper.

"Sure, Hannah told me you were only friends." Dolly winked at Hannah and the two women shared a special grin. "But after last night, or should I say this morning, I might have to rip your arms off if I catch them around any other woman."

"Dolly!" Embarrassed, Eli glanced from Hannah to Kane, seeking help.

"Don't look at me, partner," Kane chuckled. "I'd say you've got your hands full."

"Now . . ." Dolly settled her hip onto the edge of Eli's desk. "Somebody want to tell me what's going on here?"

"How much did you hear?" Eli ran a nervous hand over the back of his neck.

"Not much," she assured him. "Just something about Hannah trusting you with her life and Kane doing his job. I assume it has something to do with protecting Hannah from that scuzball in Albuquerque."

"You assume correctly." Hannah spoke up before Kane could stop her. "I'm sorry I lied to you."

Shrugging her shoulders, Dolly said, "You just did what you had to do. So what's happening now?"

"That's none of your damned business, lady," Kane ground out before turning to Eli. "Get her out of here."

"Dolly, he's right." Eli took hold of her arm and led her toward the door. "This does need to remain private."

"I'll go," Dolly held up her hand before they dismissed her entirely. "But I want your promise that you'll do whatever you have to for Hannah."

"That's what I'm trying to do," Kane said brusquely, wishing the woman would leave so they could get on with the matter at hand.

"Okay." Dolly gave Hannah a quick hug. "You let me know if you need me."

"Thanks." Hannah returned the hug and watched her new friend leave. "You didn't have to be so tacky."

"Hannah, the woman could be on Sanchez's payroll," Kane pointed out and didn't give Hannah time to argue. "Now shut up so I can figure out how to get you out of town before Sanchez and his men know where you are."

A startled cry echoed through the outer office and Eli rushed through the door, his gun ready. "Texetta, what's wrong?"

Eli returned in a few seconds holding a paper. The color had drained from his face and his voice shook as he showed them what had upset his dispatcher. "She didn't see anyone drop it off."

Hannah glanced down at the paper and accompanying photo. Someone had taped a snapshot of Devin Anderson playing in his backyard onto the paper. Beneath the picture was another mutilated nursery rhyme.

There was an old woman who lived in a shoe.
She had so many children she didn't know what to do.
She gave them some broth without any bread,
And when she turned around, they were all dead.

"Dear Lord," Hannah cried, sinking to her knees at Kane's feet. "He's threatening the children."

TEN

Dropping to her side, Kane held her for a minute. "Hannah, we're not going to let him hurt anyone. A.L. has already let the word leak that you aren't going to testify."

"But I am," she protested. "I have to, I can't let him get away with this."

"Baby, you *will* testify." Kane helped her to her feet, grateful that her anger had brought some of the color back to her cheeks. "I just want Sanchez to think that his threats are getting to you."

"Smart," was Eli's only comment.

"But this means someone is watching me." Hannah indicated the paper. "How will we get out of town without them following us?"

"I'm going to call A.L. and have him send a female agent to use as a decoy."

"How long will that take?" Eli asked, warming to the plan.

"I don't have any idea," Kane was forced to admit. "Could be a matter of hours. It might be tomorrow."

"We don't have that long," Eli insisted. "We can use Texetta."

Kane's eyebrows shot up and he glanced into the outer office. "The Dragonlady?"

"She's the closest thing we've got to a female officer," Eli pointed out. "She has had some training and I know she'd do it. Anything for Hannah."

"No, Eli," Hannah interrupted. "We can't put anyone else in danger."

"I have to agree with Hannah. There is some risk involved." Kane held the newest threat up as a reminder.

"Look, if we're careful, we can pull it off." Eli began to outline his plan for the two of them.

"It looks great on paper," Kane agreed when Eli had finished. "But let's wait for A.L. Maybe he can get someone here today and we won't have to worry about it. This," he said, pointing to Eli's detailed sketch of their plan. "This is our last resort."

Kane turned to leave Eli's office but stopped before he got to the door. "I don't guess it matters where I call from now. They know she's here."

Hannah tossed her now-cold coffee into the trash can and refilled her cup. It wasn't that she actually wanted the stuff but she had to keep busy while Kane made his call. *Is there anything more aggravating than listening to a one-sided phone conversation?* she wondered. It was impossible to tell Kane's reaction to A.L.'s reply. Was he hearing what he wanted to? Or was A.L. blowing their plan out of the water before it had a chance?

Finally, Kane hung up the phone and turned to face them. "It'll be tomorrow before he can get anyone here."

"That's too long," Eli said.

"I know." The reluctance in Kane's voice was evident. "You make sure she knows exactly what she's getting into." He nodded toward the outer office where Texetta was busy filing papers. "This isn't fun and games. These are the bad guys I'm talking about and John Wayne won't be riding down the street to the rescue."

Without a word, Eli left the office to discuss the matter with his dispatcher. By the time he returned, Hannah was a mass of guilt. When she read the fear in the older woman's eyes, Hannah was amazed that Eli could even expect her to go through with this nonsense. "Eli, I don't want her to do it."

"I'll be all right, honey," Texetta assured her. "Just as long as you're safe."

Eli and Kane both nodded at Texetta's assurance. *What is the matter with them?* Hannah wondered. *Didn't they hear the tremor in her voice or notice the way her hands shook as she clasped them in front of her?* Texetta wasn't up to this and Hannah knew she had to stop it before it went any further.

"No," Hannah declared. "There has to be another way."

"We've got to get you out of town," Kane said, pushing away from his position against the far wall and coming to stand in front of Hannah. "I don't like it, either, but we don't have any choice."

"Yes, we do," Hannah insisted. Placing her hands on Kane's chest, she begged him with her eyes. "Eli has already said his office was virtually foolproof. We can wait until tomorrow."

"By tomorrow Sanchez will know more about our plan than we do," Kane ground out, his face inches from hers. "He'll know the route we are intending to use and the location of the safe house."

"Then why are we even bothering at all." Hannah barked back, refusing to knuckle under. "Why don't I just stroll down the street and let them take pot shots at me? If he's going to get me anyway, why are we placing Texetta and Eli in danger? Why are you even here?"

"You are the most stubborn woman ever born on God's green earth!" Kane shouted, revealing his frustration at the accuracy of Hannah's words. "I don't know why I'm here. You won't listen to one word I say. You run off and get drunk. You—"

"Come on, Kane, let's calm down here and figure out a way to outmaneuver Sanchez." Eli stepped between the two lovers to prevent any further conflict. "You may not think Hannah stands a chance, but I'm not giving up."

"Who said I was giving up?" Kane demanded, turning his anger toward the sheriff. "I'm all for a good plan."

"Then let's get busy." With that, the two men swept Texetta out of the office and locked the door behind them.

"Wait!" Hannah cried, beating on the steel door. "Don't leave me in here alone!"

Knowing it was useless to continue hitting the heavy door, Hannah grabbed the phone and dialed Eli's pager number. "Get me out of here."

After waiting a few seconds, she decided they were planning to ignore her and she dialed the outside phone line. When Texetta answered, she quickly asked the older woman to plead her case. "Please don't leave me in here alone."

"I'll see what I can do, honey," Texetta promised before disconnecting.

After a few minutes, Hannah heard the lock being opened and she hurried to the door. "Thank goodness."

"Hi." Dolly peeked inside the door before stepping over the threshold. "They said I could sit in here with you for a while."

"At least it's better than staying in here alone."

"Hey!" Dolly said, pretending to be offended. "I can always leave, you know."

"Oh, Dolly, I didn't mean it the way it sounded." Hannah hugged her new friend. "I just can't stand being locked up. I have a mild case of claustrophobia and it drives me crazy to know I can't get out."

"You want to tell me just what is going on here?" Dolly popped open the small refrigerator in the corner of the office and retrieved a diet soda. "This is like something out of a spy movie. I keep expecting James Bond to saunter through the door."

"Sometimes I think we've got Laurel and Hardy instead." Hannah was in no mood to be gracious under pressure. She was furious with their casual dismissal of her ideas. "They've lost their minds, Dolly. They're planning to disguise Texetta to look like me. Eli will pose as Kane and Deputy Baker will escort them to the airport. Eli is positive that whoever is out there watching me will be fooled and follow them."

"Texetta doesn't look anything like you," Dolly pointed out.

"I know that and you know that, but I can't seem to explain it to the *superior* males out there." Hannah helped herself to a soda and flopped down in Eli's chair to stare out the window. "Sanchez has got someone out there, willing to kill me. I can't let them use Texetta."

Dolly pursed her lips as she thought over the current situation. "Let me see if I've got this straight. This Sanchez wants you dead so you can't testify against him. The bad guys are out there waiting to shoot you down and this plan of Eli's is supposed to get you safely out of town."

"Right so far."

"Eli and Texetta will take off in one direction and you and Kane will go in the other." Dolly's eyes lit up at a new thought. "Kane isn't just your lover, is he? He's an agent or something."

"Well . . ." Hannah blushed, remembering the events of the morning. "He is an agent with the DEA. He's supposed to be protecting me."

"Boy, you see cases on TV where the woman falls in love with the cop who's protecting her," Dolly grinned. "I never thought it actually happened, though."

"Our case is a little different," Hannah admitted and, in a rush, unburdened herself of the truth about Kane and his connection with her past. Even though the bond she and Dolly were forming was new, it was as solid as any she had ever felt with another woman. Dolly would understand her feelings and sympathize.

"He's your brother-in-law?" Even the worldly Dolly was shocked by the revelation. "And you've been in love with him for years?"

"Sad, isn't it?" Hannah tossed her empty can into the wastebasket and threaded her fingers together behind her neck. "It looks like our second chance won't work out any better than the first one."

"It might," Dolly offered. "I mean, he's taken care of you so far. Maybe when this is over, you two will be together."

"Anything's possible."

The door opened and the two men hurried to drop their packages on the desk. "I think we've got everything we need to fix Texetta up. We had a devil of a time finding a wig long enough, but we decided not to worry about it."

"Why not?" Hannah held up a denim skirt much like the one she was wearing.

"Sanchez and his men will expect us to use a disguise." Eli said, shaking out a pair of panty hose. "We want it to look like we have disguised you like Texetta."

"So you're going to disguise Texetta to look like me disguised as Texetta?" Hannah shook her head in confusion. "Didn't Julie Andrews make a movie like this one time?"

"This isn't make-believe, Hannah." Kane's voice was sharp, his words clipped. "Those men will use real bullets if they get the chance."

Hannah noticed all the color drain from Texetta's face and placed her hand on the woman's arm. "You don't have to do this."

"I want to," the woman assured her. "Now let's get busy."

"Hannah . . ." Eli dumped the clothing into her arms. "You and Dolly can help Texetta while Kane and I get the vehicles ready. If Baker calls in, tell him to get up here pronto."

"I'll do it," Hannah agreed. "But I won't like it."

"You don't have to like it," Kane said, following Eli out of the office and shutting the door.

After sticking her tongue out at his retreating figure, Hannah turned to the two women. "There has to be some other way."

"What about me?" Dolly volunteered. "I can do it."

"No," Hannah shook her head. "You've got the boys depending on you. This is serious stuff."

"So am I." Dolly's voice raised slightly. "Look, Hannah, you're the first friend I've had in a long time. I'm going to do whatever I can to make sure you stick around."

"I appreciate that, Dolly, but I can't let you do this," Hannah said, reaching over to squeeze the other woman's hand. "But there is something you can do for me."

"You name it."

"Take care of Eli for me." Hannah found Dolly's blush amusing. "He doesn't eat right unless someone cooks for him. I swear the man would live on peanut butter and jelly."

A sly smile curved Dolly's full lips and she uttered a low, sensual chuckle. "I think that can be arranged. There's nothing I like better than satisfying a man's . . . appetites."

"I knew I could count on you."

"Hannah, shouldn't we get started?" Texetta asked, her voice and demeanor unusually subdued.

"I guess so," Hannah admitted, still trying to think of some other way of making Kane's plan work. Unfortunately, hours of reading murder mysteries didn't prepare you for the reality. She might be able to figure out "whodunit" within the first hundred pages of the latest thriller, but she didn't have a clue how to save her own hide. It appeared she was going to have to continue to follow the rules.

The three women set about stuffing Texetta's hair into a wig that vaguely resembled Hannah's coloring and then preceded to tie a scarf around it. The skirt the men had come up with was two sizes too big for the petite woman and they used a piece of rope to hold it up. The shoes were too small and Hannah slipped out of her own loafers.

"This is ridiculous," Hannah observed, examining their creation. "She doesn't even resemble me."

They pushed and prodded and rearranged to no avail. Nothing they did made Texetta look anything like Hannah. "At least the men will have to come up with another plan," Hannah sighed, relieved that Texetta wouldn't have to go through with it.

Unfortunately, neither man commented on the obvious difference in the two women when they returned. They merely shrugged their shoulders and said it would have to do.

Dragging a disbelieving Hannah back to the cell, Kane locked her in and told her to keep her mouth shut until he came to get her. As he was heading for the door, he turned and walked back to whisper, "I am sorry."

"I don't want to be in here," she begged. "Please."

Shaking his head, Kane left the room before he could give in to her pleas. It wrenched his gut to see her staring at him through those bars, her eyes wide with fear, but it was the safest place for her. He had to keep reminding himself that if he wanted a chance at a future with her, he had to keep her alive.

"Is everything ready?" Kane asked, stepping into the outer office.

"Just got the word from Mike. The plane is fueled and on the runway. Baker's waiting out back." Eli unlocked the gun cabinet and pulled a rifle out along with two extra clips for the 9mm automatic strapped to his side. "Dolly's finishing up with Texetta."

"She better hurry."

"Texetta!" Eli called into his office. "Shake a leg, we're moving."

"Eli, I—" Kane held out his hand to the lawman. "I don't know how to thank you."

Returning the handshake, Eli said, "Just keep her safe."

With that, Kane took up his position at the front door and Eli beckoned to a heavily made-up Texetta. Grabbing the older woman's arm, he hurried her through the hallway and out the back door where a small blue pickup truck was waiting. "Jump in and keep your head down."

Wrapped from head to toe, Eli caught a glimpse of a smile on the woman's face and decided Hannah had been wrong about Texetta. Even though he couldn't see her eyes through the dark sunglasses, she was obviously having a good time. "Did you bring your gun?"

The brightly colored scarf nodded quickly and Eli revved the motor once before starting down the alley and onto the side road. Deputy Baker picked them up at the corner and they rushed through town, ignoring the myriad of people hurrying out their doors to catch a glimpse of the unusual parade.

Once Eli hit the road leading to the small airport, he pushed the foot feed almost to the floor. The small truck bounced all over the road but he managed to keep it on the pavement. "Hang on, Texetta."

A muffled groan was the only reply.

The airport was only five miles out of town and the caravan was pulling onto the runway within minutes of leaving the station. Baker had been in contact with

Kane and, sure enough, the blond surfer in Mamie's had shot out the door right after the pickup went past.

Eli helped Texetta into the waiting Cessna and settled himself behind the controls. "Looks like we made it."

The plane had already been checked by Mike Cutler, the airport manager, so Eli did away with the preflight checklist and headed the sputtering plane down the runway. "Better strap yourself in, Tex."

As the plane lifted into the air, he caught sight of a vehicle making a U-turn on the airport road and heading back to town. They had managed to outwit the man and with any luck, Kane and Hannah were already heading out of town. In the opposite direction.

"We did it, Tex." He reached over and patted her knee. "Now we just need to locate Hannah and Kane and see if they've picked up a tail."

"I hope you've got an airsick bag." The woman next to him suddenly ripped off her sunglasses and wig to reveal a green-eyed redhead about to be sick.

"Dolly!"

"What do you mean, she got away?"

"They had a plane waiting. She was surrounded all the time. I think the last note might have been too much. The security is tight." Tony flinched, expecting anger.

"It doesn't matter." Sanchez dismissed the incident. *"Get out of town. Call me in two days and I will have further instructions."*

"More notes?"

"No." Sanchez's voice was ominous. *"She's had her last warning."*

ELEVEN

"There he goes." Kane spoke into the hand-held radio connecting him with Deputy Baker. "Right on schedule. We're outta here."

"Good luck."

Slipping quickly through the office, Kane grabbed the keys from Texetta's desk and released Hannah from her prison. "Looks like we may have pulled it off."

"They got away?" Hannah asked, following Kane. Stopping as he entered the men's room, she was startled as he reached for her arm and jerked her in after him. "Kane!"

"Don't be such a prude," he ordered. With a minimum of effort he upset the trash can and placed it under the window. "This window is completely concealed by bushes."

"You expect me to climb out of *this*?" Hannah didn't really foresee an answer since he was already unlocking the exterior bars and removing them. "It's too high."

"I'll hoist you up," he promised. "Once you get through, just drop to the ground."

Opening her mouth to dispute him, Hannah tried to recall the number of times she had won an argument with Kane and decided it wasn't worth it. "Yes, dear."

Grinning at her sarcasm, Kane helped her onto the trash can and planted his shoulder under her rear end to lift her the extra few inches she needed. "Careful. I don't want you to break anything."

"Don't worry," she huffed. "I plan on surviving just so I can get my revenge."

Grabbing the hard brick edge for support, Hannah pushed through the window, head first. "How am I supposed to drop down from this position? I'll break my neck."

"Wiggle around until your feet are hanging out."

Settling her small frame sideways on the narrow ledge, Hannah managed to shove one bare foot through the window and straddle it. From there it was easier to maneuver her other leg out and jump to the ground. Her feet made contact with a thousand tiny sharp sticks from the bushes and she bit her tongue to keep from crying out. There was still a chance that Sanchez had more men out there waiting for them.

She barely had time to move out of the way before Kane dropped down beside her. "Where the hell are your shoes?"

"I gave them to Texetta," she said. "You didn't tell me we would be taking off on a cross-country trek."

"I guess we'll just have to make the best of it." Grabbing her hand, he pulled her along behind as he navigated the narrow gap between the building and the bushes.

"Ow!" she wailed, stubbing her toe on the brick wall. "Slow down."

"I can't." But he did diminish his pace so she could be more careful where she stepped. "The car is about four blocks away. Keep your head down and do exactly what I tell you."

"What are you going to tell me?" she asked, imitating his posture as they slipped along the back of the sheriff's office and across the alley.

"To shut up," he ordered, zigging through a neighboring backyard.

The weight of the flak jacket caused Hannah to stumble in her efforts to simulate Kane's graceful movements. Her feet were aching from running across the rock-filled alley and straight into the sticker patch Harley Jamison called a backyard. "Can't we run on the sidewalk?"

"Give me your foot," he ordered when she stopped to pluck out the stickers. With a gentleness he was far from feeling at that particular moment, he deftly slid the offending thorns from her foot. Crouching down on one knee, he placed her arms around his neck. "Hold on."

"I'm too heavy," she protested when she realized he meant to carry her. "I'll be okay."

"I thought I told you to shut up."

Wrapping her arms around his neck, Hannah clung to his broad back as he hurried the remaining blocks to where Texetta had parked her van. She almost wept with relief at the sight of the comfortable navy vehicle waiting on the corner. "How will we get it back to her?"

"Hannah . . ." Kane shook his head at her question.

"Let's concentrate on getting you out of here alive before we worry about the damned car."

Hopping in as he opened the door, Hannah started
to buckle her seat belt. Deciding to remove the heavy
jacket first, she was startled when Kane's hand clamped
down on hers. "What now?"

"You ride in back." He jerked his thumb toward the
back of the van. "And keep that jacket on."

"But—"

"Shut up, Hannah," he said wearily. "For once just
do what I tell you without any discussion."

"Fine," she huffed and settled onto the makeshift
bed in the extreme back of the van. She couldn't see
why he got so upset with her. She was doing her best.
Could she help it if she didn't know anything about
making a getaway?

Maintaining her silence as Kane took the back roads
out of town, Hannah allowed the gentle rocking of the
van to lull her into a fitful slumber. Her body needed
the release of a peaceful sleep, but her mind was too
wired to relax.

Instead of falling into a deep, restful nap, she was
tormented by dreams of Sanchez capturing Eli and Texetta. The startling reality of her nightmare brought her
fully awake and she sat up on the bed.

Through the window she could see that they were
traveling northwest toward Portales. Was that where
the safe house was located? Would Kane's contacts be
waiting for them with an entire army assigned to keep
her safe? "How much longer?"

"Did you have a good nap?" Kane asked over the
muted sound of the radio.

"Not especially." Yawning, she moved from the bed

to the seat directly behind Kane. "When will we get there?"

"In about fifteen minutes," he said, switching lanes and picking up speed.

"Is there something wrong?" she asked, leaning over to watch the speedometer top eighty-five miles an hour.

"Not a thing." He flicked on the blinker and returned to the right-hand lane. Deciding to put an end to her curiosity, he explained. "By switching lanes and varying my speed I can tell if someone is following us."

"What if the highway patrol pulls us over?"

He caught her reflection in the rearview mirror and grinned. "Hannah, I don't think we need to worry about getting a ticket."

"Would you stop making fun of me!" she cried, crossing her arms over her chest and settling back in the seat. "I haven't spent years doing stuff like this, you know. I can't help it if I happen to ask perfectly normal questions. When I speed, I worry about getting caught. If I borrow a friend's car, I'm concerned about getting it back to them in one piece."

"Hannah . . ." he began, but she didn't hear him.

"You people should write a book on proper witness protocol," she continued, venting her frustration. "*How to Send the Bad Guys to Jail and Stay Alive.* You could write chapters on disguises and how to lose a tail. At least then I might have some idea of what was going on."

"I know it's hard to blindly follow orders." The soft tone of his voice pierced her anger. "I just don't always have time to give you an explanation for everything. Just trust me."

"Oh, Kane," she said, suddenly contrite. "I do trust

you. I'm just having a hard time with all this. It's hard to believe that there are men out there waiting to kill me.''

Kane reached his hand behind the seat and Hannah grabbed it. Squeezing her fingers, he promised, ''I'll get you out of this, baby.''

''I know.''

Any further conversation was postponed as Kane abruptly swung the van off the main highway onto a dirt road. A few yards off the road was an old barn that looked as if a stiff wind could blow it away. Kane drove the van into the barn and shut off the motor. ''Now we wait.''

''For A.L.?'' she asked, coming to sit in the front seat.

''No,'' he said, preventing her from sitting down. ''Get back there.''

''Come with me,'' she cajoled, thinking of his safety.

''I have to keep a lookout,'' he explained. ''If we were being followed and they were on to us, they'll turn in here. If they didn't see us turn off, the dirt road would send up a flare.''

''So we wait until they find us or go past,'' she surmised. Some of his actions were beginning to make sense. Or maybe her mind was becoming as warped as his. ''What do we do if they turn in?''

''Don't worry about it,'' he commented absently. His eyes were trained on the steady stream of cars traveling north.

''Stop it!'' Her anger was once again on the rise. ''If I know what to expect, I'll at least stand a fighting chance. Don't shut me out of this, Kane. Seth shut me out of *everything*. If I had known even a little about his life, I wouldn't have been so shocked by what happened."

"He probably didn't want you to sit around and worry." Kane's eyes left the road for a second to meet hers. "Sometimes ignorance is bliss."

"And some people are blistered," Hannah finished her grandmother's favorite quote. "I didn't want to know everything he was doing. But . . . at the end . . . he excluded me completely. I didn't even know he was working on the task force."

Shifting around in the front seat so that he could keep an eye on the highway, Kane sought something to say. He understood his brother's reasons for not letting Hannah become involved in his work. Over the years Kane had seen too many marriages fall by the wayside because the wife couldn't handle the constant danger. If Hannah had been aware of the immediate threat to Seth's life, it would have made her miserable. "Hannah, I'm sure Seth was only thinking of you."

"Maybe," she admitted, but her heart wasn't in it. Seth had been like a little boy with a secret. He would occasionally drop hints as to the nature of his work, but he never actually came out and said he was becoming involved in undercover work. As far as Hannah knew, he was merely riding around in a car with his partner.

After the incident in the parking lot, Hannah had been embarrassed to admit she had no idea of what her husband's life was like. It had been a rude awakening to discover that the other wives were all much more aware of what their men did after leaving the house every morning. "Maybe it was just another aspect of his life that I had no part in."

"Damn, Hannah," Kane snapped, his control quickly

reaching the breaking point. "Seth did what he thought was best. You can't know what it was like for him, so just hush. He loved you, isn't that enough?"

Tears sprang to Hannah's eyes and her teeth clamped down on her quivering bottom lip. She hadn't meant to insinuate that Seth didn't love her, or that she didn't appreciate the nature of his work. She had thought Kane might be a sympathetic ear for all of the little nagging thoughts and emotions she had been carrying around for the past year and a half.

Had it been her fault that Seth wouldn't share his opinions and feelings? Had he felt she was too big a wimp to handle the knowledge of his job? Didn't he think she loved him enough to stand beside him whatever decision he made?

That one continued to haunt her. Seth had been openly affectionate and it bothered him that she preferred to keep her emotions inside. How many times had he tried to wrap his arm around her while they were walking and she shrugged it off? Would it have killed her to let him kiss her in public? Would anyone really have been offended by the sight of a young couple showing their love for each other?

She had tried to explain to Seth that she wasn't comfortable with public shows of affection. She certainly hadn't been shy in the bedroom, or the living room, or the kitchen, or anywhere else the mood struck. As long as it was in private and away from prying eyes and wagging tongues she was as sexually liberated as the next woman. But years of growing up in Hanson, where even walking down the street holding hands was frowned upon, had repressed her to a certain extent.

The sound of the motor tore her from her musings and she automatically replaced her seat belt as Kane left the ramshackle building to head down the dirt road. Evidently they weren't being followed. She wanted to ask a hundred questions about what she should expect, but the tension in the car was too high. Kane would just bite her head off again.

"We're almost there." Kane watched for her reaction in the rearview mirror and was surprised when she merely nodded her understanding. He had been prepared to answer at least half a dozen questions concerning the safe house. "A.L. will be waiting."

Another nod.

"Is anything wrong?"

"No," she answered softly. "I'm okay. I trust you."

"Good." At least he was finally getting what he wanted—a docile Hannah. She should trust him. There was no reason for him to explain his every action or the reasons behind such action. He was trained to take care of her. That was all she needed to know.

So why did her silence bother him so much? He finally had what he wished for and it turned out to be the wrong wish. Just his luck. "I didn't mean to snap at you a while ago, I'm just not used to having to answer to anyone. I've been alone too long to be any good at conversation."

Before she had a chance to reply the van bumped over a small hill in the road and the safe house came into view. Nestled among a small dotting of trees, the farmhouse had the advantage of being surrounded by acres of open flat land. There were no nearby gullies or ravines for concealment, only a small rise to the west. The brick structure looked sturdy.

A.L. must have already seen them coming because he was stepping off the front porch. Another man followed him through the gate and they stood waiting until Kane pulled to a stop directly beside them.

"Took you long enough," A.L. said by way of greeting. "Our spotter had you almost all the way, but you ditched him a few miles back."

"I planned it that way." Kane held out his hand to shake A.L.'s and then offered it to the other man. "Jason, it's good to see you."

"McCord." Jason Dreyer enthusiastically returned the handshake. "I always said you would come back from the dead for this."

Glancing down at the paper Jason had slipped into his palm, a grin spread across Kane's face. "Actually, I had forgotten about loaning you this." He held the twenty up to inspect it. "This wouldn't be fake, would it?"

"No way," Jason chuckled.

"Kane?" All three men turned in the direction of the van.

"You can come out, Hannah." Kane had a suspicion this new Hannah was going to get on his nerves.

Tugging her jacket around her, Hannah cautiously made her way to stand directly behind Kane. He wanted an obedient simpleton? She'd give it to him in spades.

"Hannah, this is A.L. Hardaway." Kane waited until she raised her eyes to acknowledge the man before introducing Jason. "Jason will be staying at the house with us."

"It's nice to meet you, ma'am." Jason reached for Hannah's hand and held it gently in his. "We'll take good care of you."

Hannah tilted her head up to smile at the sweet-faced man. "Thank you, Jason."

"Do you have any bags?" Jason asked, heading for

the van. Within a few minutes he was leading Hannah up the stone sidewalk into the house, leaving Kane and A.L. behind.

"Old Jason is still a ladykiller," A.L. commented, watching the two of them enter the house. "It's a good thing he isn't married or we couldn't let him work cases like this."

"He can just stay the hell away from her," Kane ground out, stalking up the path Hannah had just trod.

"Oh, so that's the way it is "

"The way what is?" Kane thrust open the front door, his eyes searching for Hannah and that middle-aged Lothario.

"You and Hannah," A.L. said, pointing in the direction of the stairway.

"I don't know what you are talking about," Kane insisted, taking the stairs two at a time. "She's my sister-in-law and she's in trouble. That's it."

Watching Kane barge into the room that had been assigned to Hannah, A.L. decided Hannah wasn't the only one in trouble. He had known Kane McCord for thirteen years and never once had he seen his friend's emotions so close to the surface. He almost wished he could stick around to watch the show.

"I'll take it from here, Dreyer." Kane's words abruptly cut off Hannah's laughter at one of Jason's jokes as they unpacked her things and the two jumped apart. "I don't want her to leave this room."

"I don't think that's necessary," Jason argued, but the look in Kane's eyes caused him to back down. "Okay, we'll do it your way."

"Damned right we will." Jerking Hannah's clothing from Jason's hands, he tossed them onto the bed. "Finish unpacking while we get things worked out. I'll be up to check on you later.''

Nodding, Hannah gave Jason a shy smile. ''Thank you for helping. I'm sure I'll see you later.''

''You will if I have anything to say about it,'' Jason promised, heading for the door.

''You don't.'' Kane reminded him and turned to face Hannah. ''Don't encourage him. I need his mind on his job, not your underwear.'' He indicated the pair of lace panties lying on the bed.

Refusing to blush, Hannah merely nodded before saying, ''At least it's gratifying to know someone's mind is on my underwear.''

TWELVE

"It's just not fair." Jason's full lips turned down as he tallied Hannah's winnings. They had spent the better part of the last three days playing cards and Jason now owed Hannah around twenty thousand dollars. "Aw, well, unlucky in cards—lucky in love."

"Hah!" Hannah gloated. "Luck, my aunt Fanny, it was pure skill. Just be glad we're only playing on paper."

Leaning across the table, Jason grabbed her hands as they shuffled the cards. "I could be your indentured servant until I pay my IOU." His voice was low and Hannah had the impression he wasn't entirely joking.

"The way you're losing," Hannah teased, pulling her hands from his, "I'll be an old woman before you pay me back." The heated look in his pale-green eyes made her uncomfortable.

"I've had enough cards for today," Jason's good mood vanished as he shoved away from the card table set up in the corner of Hannah's room. "I need a walk. Care to join me?"

"And risk the wrath of Kane?" Hannah shook her head and dealt herself a hand of solitaire. "You go ahead, though. Thanks for keeping me company."

"Anytime, pretty lady." With an exaggerated wink, he strolled from the room.

Hannah heard the muted thud of his steps as he quickly made his way down the stairs. Within seconds the front door popped open and she could hear him conversing with Kane. What were they talking about this time? Or rather, *arguing* about? Her?

In the three days since their arrival, Hannah had yet to figure out the strange relationship between Kane and Jason Dreyer. On the surface they seemed to be old friends with a wealth of history bonding them together, but occasionally, Hannah spied something deeper. An inner battle between the two men that scared her.

Jason's laughter had a brittle edge to it that made it seem almost maniacal. He was a good-looking, witty, intelligent man most of the time. It was only in rare unguarded moments that Hannah sensed an underlying sadness. A hurt that he almost succeeded in hiding. Had Hannah not experienced her own personal sorrow, she might not have recognized it in Jason. It was in his eyes whenever he caught her looking at Kane. Hadn't he ever had a woman look at him through the eyes of love?

"Queen of diamonds on king of spades," a masculine voice said over her shoulder.

"A.L.!" Hannah dropped the stack of cards she had been idly shuffling and spun round in her chair. "You scared me to death."

"Sorry." His apology was sincere. "I thought you heard me come in."

"No," she answered, gathering the cards to hide her nervousness. The truth was, her heart was still pounding from his unexpected appearance. Jumping at every sound had become a way of life—a legacy from Sanchez. "I was daydreaming. When did you get back?"

"Just now." Grabbing the heavily marked score pad by her elbow, he chuckled. "Has Jason given you his 'unlucky in cards' speech yet?"

"Yes, actually," Hannah grinned, grateful for A.L.'s return. Maybe with him around to run interference between Kane and Jason the atmosphere around the house wouldn't be so tense. She had expected A.L. to stay with them, but Kane explained that he was their outside man. He only dropped in every few days to check on them. "He's such a tease."

"Sometimes," was his cryptic reply. "How are you holding up?"

"Don't expect me to lie and say fine," she warned, rising from her chair and walking to peek out the window. She reached up to carefully part the slats of the miniblinds. Kane was constantly reminding her to stay away from the windows, but every now and then she had to have a glimpse of the real world.

Although her room was comfortable and she had been supplied with everything from books to a video game, she still saw it for what it was—a tastefully decorated prison. "I hate this, A.L. Kane won't even let me go downstairs."

"I know it's hard," he sympathized, coming to stand behind her. He took her shoulders in his large hands and began to massage the taut muscles of her neck. "But I do have some good news."

"What?" Whirling around, her nose made contact with his chin and they both laughed. That was how Kane found them.

"Damn, A.L., not you, too." Striding across the bedroom, he grabbed Hannah's arm and pulled her from A.L.'s loose embrace. "I've spent the last three days trying to keep Dreyer from attacking her—and now you."

"Slow down, old man," A.L. grinned. "I just came up here to tell Hannah that we caught the man who was leaving the notes."

"That's great!" Hannah automatically turned to Kane. "Does that mean I can go home?"

"No," they answered in unison.

"Hannah, they caught *one* man," Kane explained. "You won't be safe until after the trial."

Pasting a smile on her face to keep them from knowing how upset she was, Hannah nodded. "I understand." Turning to A.L., she asked, "Did you bring me any more books?"

"Got a whole sackful in the car," he said and prepared to leave. "I did your shopping, too, McCord."

"Did you get everything?"

"Everything but the pasta maker. Do you have any idea how much those things cost?"

"Pasta maker?" Hannah asked, once A.L. left the room.

"I thought you might want to cook." Shrugging his shoulders, Kane's expression told Hannah not to make too much of his thoughtfulness. "I'm tired of eating Dreyer's slop."

If there was one thing Hannah had learned in the last three days, it was that Kane McCord was in love with her. Or so very nearly so it didn't matter. He didn't want to be—heck, he probably didn't even know he was. But she knew, and it was enough for now.

The fact that he had sent A.L. out shopping for cooking supplies only emphasized how much he wanted to please her. He could hide behind his scowl and say it was because Jason couldn't cook, but he didn't fool her.

Just like he had accidentally *found* that stack of paperback romances for her on their first day in the safe house. Jason had readily volunteered the truth on that little matter. Kane had told A.L. to stock up on the novels when they were setting up the protection. Who else but a man in love would bother to find out her favorite authors?

"The kitchen is downstairs." Hannah turned back to the window to watch A.L. unload the supplies. "Does this mean I actually get to leave this room?"

"Only when I'm with you." Jamming his hands into the back pockets of his jeans, Kane refused to admit this cold-fish routine was driving him crazy. "I'll escort you to the kitchen and stay with you while you cook. You'll have to eat there." A grin tugged at his dimple as he saw a storm brewing in the honey depths of her eyes. At last—some spark of life. For three days she had been about as much fun as a root canal. Sure, he was the one who kept telling her to shut up, but he hadn't thought she would really do it.

"Fine." The flash in her eyes died as quickly as it came to life. "Just let me know when you're ready."

"Hannah . . ." Kane ventured a step closer to the suddenly frail woman. Who was this mousy creature who refused to argue? He knew his words from the other day had hurt her, but he hadn't thought he would kill her spirit entirely. "I know this is hard."

"It isn't your fault," she said without a shred of emotion. "You're only doing your job."

"That's right." Angered by her quiet acquiescence, he stomped from the room. "I'll be back in a few minutes. And stay away from the window."

Wincing as he slammed the door, Hannah raised her hand to cover the grin that threatened to ruin her award-winning performance. If her calculations were correct, she would have driven Kane beyond his endurance by the end of the day—tomorrow afternoon, at the latest.

What started out as hurt feelings by his abrupt attitude had slowly evolved into a plan. Kane claimed he didn't want anyone in his life. He was too set in his ways to change, especially for a woman. But Hannah suspected that was exactly what he wanted—and needed.

So she would give him the Hannah he asked for—quiet, unassuming, subservient. She might be walking the ragged edge of insanity before he came to his senses, but it would be worth it.

Taking the time to tuck her white oxford shirt into the waistband of her faded jeans, she slipped into her tennis shoes and waited. Sure enough, within a few minutes, Kane was knocking at the door.

Giving in to the need for an outlet for her excitement at being released from her cage, Hannah whirled around with her hands in the air before opening the door. Despite the rush of freedom pumping through her, she managed to present the calmly detached facade she had perfected over the last few days. "Thank you."

"You're welcome," he grumbled beside her. Taking her arm, he pulled her behind him as he led her down the stairs. "Stay behind me and never step in front of the window."

"Yes, sir." Leaning closer to him, she pressed herself against the length of his back. She didn't know if he was affected by her maneuver, but her own temperature was definitely on the rise. "Like this?"

"Not so . . ." His breath caught slightly in his throat. "Close."

"Okay," she whispered against the back of his neck as he took the next step down, his back sliding along her front in the process. "Is this better?" she asked, not moving an inch.

"Fine," he said, taking the next two steps in rapid succession. Hannah had to hurry to keep up with him. "This is why I don't want you down here." He indicated a large picture window in the living room. "You're going to have to crawl across the floor until you reach the kitchen door."

"Whatever." Dropping quickly to her knees, she began the journey across the room. Waiting for Kane to take up his position behind her, she began what she hoped was the sexiest crawl in history. "Am I doing all right?"

"Hell, Hannah." Kane's voice was suddenly loud. "Just crawl."

Watching the gentle roll and twitch of her denim-covered backside was his undoing. Who would have thought a crawling woman could be so sexy? With each shift of her knees, he was subjected to another sway of her hips and it was all he could do not to reach out and take a bite of what she was offering. "Can't you go any faster? We'll be lucky if we're there by midnight."

"Okay." Glad she wasn't facing him, Hannah gave in to a grin at his discomfort. Moving slightly faster, she reached the kitchen door and waited patiently until Kane told her she could stand up.

"Dreyer!" Kane called through the door before allowing Hannah to open it. "We're coming in."

"All clear."

Shoving open the swinging kitchen door, Kane pushed Hannah into the kitchen and stepped in immediately behind her. "A.L., did you get the jacket?"

A sense of foreboding flooded through Hannah at the mention of a jacket. Surely he wasn't going to make her wear that awful flak jacket again, was he? She had been pleasantly surprised when he hadn't required her to wear it for their trek downstairs. She should have known it would be waiting for her.

Stifling a groan at the sight of A.L. advancing with the hideous thing, Hannah bit her tongue and calmly held out her arms. "How thoughtful." She smiled at A.L. as he helped her into the jacket. "Did you say something, Kane?"

"I'll be back in a few minutes." Kane's abrupt departure left both of the men staring at each other in bewilderment.

Delighting in another small victory, Hannah turned to her bodyguards and smiled. "Now, what are we having tonight, gentlemen?"

Kane slammed his fist into the back of the overstuffed sofa on his way to the front door. Once out in the chilly November night, he vented his frustration on an old tire lying just off the porch. His toes were sore but at least he was beyond the desire to paddle Hannah's perfect little backside. "She's gonna drive me to drink."

"I must be psychic." A.L. stepped out the front door and handed Kane an ice-cold beer. "Want to talk about it?"

Popping the top on the can, Kane allowed the bitter liquid to slide down his throat before answering. "Nothin' to talk about."

"Okay."

Flinging the half-full can into an old rusty trash barrel just off the porch, Kane settled his long frame on the front step for a second before jumping up to pace along the walkway. "You don't know what it's like, man. She's nuts."

"Yeah, I could see that about her right away." Leaning against the porch railing, A.L. grinned at his friend's dilemma.

"I'm serious," Kane insisted, hearing the laughter in A.L.'s words. "One minute I think I've finally got her convinced that her life is in danger and the next she's doing her best to—"

"Don't stop just when it's getting interesting," A.L. pleaded. "What's been going on out here, anyway?"

"Not a damned thing." Kane gave the tire a kick for emphasis.

"So that's the problem, huh?" Tossing down the rest of his beer, he crunched the can under his heel and threw it away. "Want some time alone?"

"You know I can't put her in that position." Even as he said the words, he thought of a dozen positions he'd like to get her in. Mentally chastising his own lack of self-control, he grabbed a handful of rocks from the edge of the walkway and began tossing them into the darkness.

"I could get Dreyer involved in a card game later," A.L. offered. "That's about the best we can do right now."

"Hell!" Kane rounded on his friend, unable to believe he was actually considering the idea. "Quit acting like I'm some horny teenager. I'm only here for her safety—*nothing else!*"

"Whatever you say, man."

"Let's change the subject," Kane ordered, his eyes automatically scouting the darkness surrounding them. He was so used to living on the edge of danger it never occurred to him that the still, purple night was simply there for his enjoyment. Enemies lurked in the dark. Deals went down and plans went sour. He rarely trusted what was in plain sight and never what was hidden. Like a machine without a turn-off switch, Kane McCord was on alert every second.

Except when he was with Hannah.

When Hannah laughed, he could believe in the goodness of the sunlight. Her eyes were warm pools of honey where he could bathe the soreness of his soul. In her arms he found safety from those hidden evils lurking in his mind. He had done the one thing that had rendered him useless in her protection—he had fallen in love with her.

"If ya'll want any of this chow, you better come on," Jason called from the front door. He didn't wait for a reply before hurrying back to the kitchen.

"If he doesn't leave her alone—" Kane didn't need to finish the threat. Both men knew that Kane wouldn't be able to stand Jason's flirtations much longer. His feelings for Hannah were too new, too uncontrollable, to allow much room for interference at this point.

"That offer still stands," A.L. said, holding the door open for Kane to precede him. "You know Jason can't resist a card game."

"Thanks, buddy." Kane slapped A.L. on the back as they made their way toward the kitchen and the enticing aroma of Hannah's cooking. "Some other time."

Dinner passed without much conversation save Jason's. While Hannah was grateful for his witty stories, she couldn't help but notice how he manipulated the evening. Kane and A.L. seemed content to let him rattle on about the cases they had worked in the past, neither offering more than a word or two when called upon for confirmation. Only when Jason brought up a woman named Gloria, did A.L. suddenly spring to life and divert the subject. Although he managed to keep them laughing, Hannah easily picked up on the new tension between the three men.

Who was this Gloria and why was A.L. so desperate to keep her out of the conversation? Had there been recognition in Kane's eyes? Was she an old lover? A *new* lover? The perfectly prepared steak turned to shoe leather in her mouth and she struggled to finish what was on her plate.

She had blamed Kane's reluctance to get involved on his guilt about Seth and his determination to protect her, but what if she had been wrong? What if Gloria was the reason Kane was so dead set against becoming involved?

"I'm ready to go back upstairs."

Three heads turned in her direction and from the look on their faces it was obvious she had shocked them with her request.

"Already?" Kane asked, a hint of suspicion darkening his eyes. "Are you okay?"

"I'm fine," she insisted, wearily. "I just want to go back upstairs. Jason, would you take me, please?"

"Your wish is my command," he said, pulling her chair out for her. His eyes locked with Kane's for a split second and a grin curved his full lips. "Ya'll can clean up the kitchen."

"Like hell," Kane snarled and was halfway out of his chair when A.L.'s hand grabbed the back of his shirt and held him in place. "I'll be right up to check on you."

"I'm going to bed and read for a while." Hannah hoped Kane would get the message. She needed to be alone to digest these new feelings. Jealousy was something she had never experienced before and it was an overwhelming emotion.

Kane watched Jason place a protective hand on the small of Hannah's waist and had a vivid fantasy of what that hand would look like nailed to the wall. "Stay away from the widow."

Hannah and Jason turned in one accord to stare at Kane. "What did you say?" Hannah asked when her mind began to function again.

"I said to stay away from the window," Kane answered, completely unaware of his previous blunder. "It puts you in a vulnerable position."

"Hell, McCord, quit telling me how to do my job," Jason growled before propelling Hannah through the kitchen door and into the living room. "His damned superior attitude is starting to get on my nerves," he said once they were making their way toward the stairs.

"This is hard on him." Hannah was immediately on the defensive. Even though she was equally irritated by Kane's attitude, she couldn't stand to hear anyone else criticize him. "He likes to be in control."

"Sometimes control can be a man's undoing." Jason held open her bedroom door and, cautioning her to wait in the hall, made a quick check of the room. "It's clear."

Doing a survey of her own, she was satisfied that everything was as she had left it. This new facet of her life was quickly becoming second nature and she could understand how Kane had become the man he was. It also helped her gain a better perception of Seth. Maybe he hadn't meant to leave her out of his life? It was possible that his job had become so much a part of him that he never even realized he was leaving her behind.

"Thank you, Jason." Hannah stopped just inside the door, preventing him from following her in. Although she liked him, she wanted time alone with her thoughts. "I'll see you in the morning."

The playful glimmer in Jason's eyes dimmed, but he didn't argue. Tugging on the end of her braid, he winked and was gone.

Hannah made quick work of slipping out of her clothes and into the white eyelet gown she had brought along. The sack of new books was resting on the edge of her mattress and she carefully selected one of the thick paperbacks before dumping the rest into the far corner of the room. She had been averaging two to three books a day since their arrival and this new batch wouldn't hold her more than a week.

A week. A.L. had informed her at dinner tonight that they would be moving her closer to Albuquerque next Monday and then into the city on Wednesday. The trial was scheduled to start on Wednesday. Seven days. If she could survive the next week, she could sit on the witness stand and tell the world what Roberto Sanchez had done to Seth. And to her.

She slid between the crisp white sheets and opened her book. Her eyes ran over the words on the page but her mind was too busy projecting the future. One scenario after another played through her head, each more farfetched than the last. She must have finally drifted off to sleep because it was daylight when she heard it!

THIRTEEN

"You lousy son of a bitch!"

Hannah sat upright in bed, clutching the sheet to her breast. She immediately recognized the voice as belonging to Kane and it caused goosebumps to rise along her back. Loathing dripped from every syllable of the curse and the series of loud smacks that followed could only be flesh hitting flesh.

More shouting had Hannah scurrying across the chilly floor toward the door. A loud crash, trailed by the resumed cacophony of a fistfight, stopped her from actually turning the knob. What if Sanchez was down there? No, she recognized the other voice. It was Jason's. Somehow she wasn't surprised that their mutual distrust of each other had led to this.

Grasping the wall for support, she found herself holding her breath as she inched along the hallway and down the first few steps. The scuffle was immediately below her. Crouching down, she peered through the slats of the banister and cringed at the violence before her.

Kane was holding Jason up by his shirtfront, his fist smashing again and again into the dazed man's face. Even from her perch, Hannah could see Kane had lost any sense of control. Whatever had transpired between them had pushed him over the edge.

"I ought to kill you." Kane seemed oblivious to everything but imposing his will on the man standing in front of him. His eyes never flickered in Hannah's direction as she crept to the bottom of the stairwell.

Jason managed to ward off the next blow and deliver one of his own to Kane's midsection. "All I did was make one lousy phone call. Maybe you've forgotten what it's like to be a man, but some of us can still get—"

Jason's words were cut off as Kane's fist smashed into his jaw, lifting him several inches from the floor. Another quick blow to his stomach and Jason fell in a heap at Kane's feet. "Get out of here, Dreyer."

In a split second, Dreyer had risen to his feet and was holding a small gun in his shaking fist. "I ought to use it."

"Go ahead," Kane challenged. His face was already swollen and bruised, but he didn't flinch under Jason's threat. His breathing was erratic as he stood before his enemy. He couldn't have made a better target.

"No!" Hannah ran across the room and threw herself into Kane's arms before either man realized she was present. Catching her in his embrace, Kane immediately pushed her behind him. "Stop this before someone gets killed!"

"Don't interfere!" Jason warned. His own breath was coming in pained gasps as he watched them. A look of pure pity filled his eyes when he gazed at Hannah. "You don't know what kind of man he is."

"Yes, I do," she said calmly, hoping to still the anger she felt in the room. Using the soft, cooing voice she employed to quiet a frightened or injured child, she continued to hold Jason's gaze. With slow, careful movements she shifted until she was standing next to Kane, her hand pressed against his rock-hard abdomen. "He's the man I love, Jason. Please don't hurt him."

An anguished cry tore from the battered man's lips and he waved the gun wildly. "No! You can't love him. He doesn't deserve a woman like you."

Hannah dared a glimpse at Kane and sucked in a harsh breath. Tanned flesh was stretched taut over the hard angles of his face and those blue eyes glittered like diamonds. His shirt was torn open, exposing the sculpted muscles of his chest. He was a stranger living in the body of the man she loved. She was both frightened and fascinated by the picture he presented.

Without saying another word, he set out to finish what he started. A slight flexing of the muscles in his right arm was all the warning Jason had before the gun was knocked from his hand and he was flat on his back. Kane towered over him. "Don't worry, I won't kill you. I hate the damned paperwork too much." Reaching down, he jerked the still man to his feet and propelled him toward the front door. After sparing Hannah a look that effectively rooted her to the spot in the middle of the living room, he stalked out the door.

From the small window on the right-hand side of the door, she could see Jason stumble off the porch in the direction of the makeshift garage. Within minutes, a nondescript blue sedan was sailing past the house leaving a wall of dirt behind. Jason was gone.

"Get back upstairs." Kane's voice came from the

porch. All the anger was gone and in its place she could detect an underlying sadness.

"What happened, Kane?" Hannah stepped onto the porch. She could see the trail of dust following Jason's departure and knew there would be serious ramifications from the events of the morning. Making her way to the edge of the porch, she reached out a shaking hand as he came to stand below her on the steps. It was odd to be taller than him and she felt strengthened by their positions. "What's going on?"

"Forget it," he ordered, taking her hand. The anger was gone, leaving him drained. "Dreyer and I just had a difference of opinion."

"I'd say that's putting it mildly." Swaying slightly in his direction, she was surprised when he suddenly wrapped his arms around her waist and buried his face in the soft, welcoming valley of her breasts. It was the first time since arriving at the safe house that he had gone willingly into her arms and she sensed that his defenses were crumbling. Smoothing his hair with her hand, she kissed the wildly disarrayed tresses. "Are you hurt?"

Shaking his head, he tightened his hold on her. "Don't worry about it, baby. It's not the first time Dreyer and I have gone at it." Hannah could feel his hand patting the small of her back as one might comfort a child. She had a vision of his mother rocking him as an infant, her hand gently stroking his back.

"It isn't?" Curiosity was getting the better of her good intentions. "Does it have something to do with Gloria?"

Stepping out of the circle of her arms, his eyes clearly showed his confusion. There was no alarm or suspicion in his voice. "What do you know about her?"

"Nothing," she said, shrugging her shoulders. The movement caused her to remember she was standing there in her nightgown and she wrapped her arms around her waist. "I just noticed A.L. seemed upset when her name came up at dinner last night."

"Yeah," he said, taking her hand and pulling her into the house behind him. "Gloria Botello is a file clerk Jason's got the hots for. A.L. caught him using the company line to sweet talk her the other day. He called her again this morning."

"And that's a problem?"

"Damn right," he said, leading her up the stairs and into the bedroom. "Any contact with the outside world puts you in danger."

"Oh." What else was there to say?

She watched him peer through the miniblinds before turning to face her again. "I have to stay up here with you until A.L. sends someone to replace Dreyer."

Taking slow, careful steps toward him, Hannah paused to consider the thought rolling around in her head. Now that they were alone, did they have enough time to kiss and make up for all the hurtful things they had said this past week? Would he reject her again on the grounds of her protection? "How long do we have?"

His eyes followed her every movement. She knew immediately when he realized her intent. "Hannah, what do you think you're doing?"

"I'm going back to bed," she answered. Her voice held none of the anxiety that ricocheted through her mind. Turning just before she reached him, she made her way to the large bed. It was still rumpled from her restless night and she took a second to smooth the sheets.

"Don't you think you should get dressed?" His voice grew deeper the second she raised the hem of her gown to reveal almost the entire length of her legs as she crawled onto the mattress. "We could play cards."

Stretching, Hannah snuggled back against the pillows. "I know a better game. Do you want to play with me?"

Growling at the suggestion in her words, he grinned. "Am I gonna like this game?"

She puckered her lips in what she hoped was a sexy pout and reached up to untie the ribbon at the base of her braid. With determined fingers she released her hair from its confines and shook it out. Long silken strands flowed across her shoulders, concealing the gentle curve of her breast. "I guess that depends on how well you play."

With a resigned sigh, Kane slowly approached the bed. From the look in his eyes as he watched her, Hannah knew he didn't have the strength to fight. He would probably curse her and stay away for days, but she knew he was curious. They both needed to find out just how strong their attraction was and if the other morning had been a fluke. Would they touch each other as deeply as they had the first time? Or would they discover that what they felt was only leftover passion from a forbidden memory?

Releasing the buttons on his jeans, Kane quickly divested himself of his clothing and slid between the sheets next to her. "I'm not sure I know the rules of this game," he whispered against her ear. "But I'm willing to learn."

Shivering in anticipation, Hannah turned her head

until her lips were against his. Catching his breath with her own, she reveled in possessing even that part of him. "It doesn't have any rules. You just make them up as you go along."

"Then I won't be cheating if I do this?" In one fluid motion he pinned her against the mattress and insinuated himself between her legs. The heated hardness of his body told her this would be no leisurely exploration. Whether it was anger at not being able to restrain himself or just an intense desire for her, Kane was playing this game all out—no punches pulled.

"No!" she gasped as his tongue traced the outline of her nipple through the thin material of her gown. "That's . . . not . . . cheating."

"How about this?" His hands began to move across her body, drawing pleasured sighs from her parted lips. "Or this?"

"No," she cried as his fingers teased her. She was too caught up in the sensations he was creating to even try to reciprocate. With love filling every corner of her heart, she wallowed in his seduction. There would be no losers in this game.

"I have one question, though," he chuckled as she clutched him to her in a frenzy of desire. "How do I score?"

The sun was hanging low in the sky by the time Hannah decided to leave her bed. She had declared Kane the victor in their little game and given in to her body's need for sleep. Without shadows from the past crowding her dreams, she was able to rest peacefully.

A little too peacefully, she decided, upon awakening to find the other side of the bed empty. Her lips curved into a lazy, satisfied grin as she recalled snuggling against her man before drifting off. *Her man*. What a wonderful phrase.

"Kane?" she called, slipping into fresh underwear and tugging a dark-green sweater over her head. Her jeans were hopelessly crumpled, so she pulled her forest-green corduroy skirt and white eyelet slip out of the closet.

Opening the bedroom door, she yelled down the stairs, but received no answer. *Where was he?* Disregarding his previous instructions about remaining in her bedroom, she quietly made her way down the stairs and into the living room.

The window in the living room showed her the last pink-and-orange rays of the sun as it drifted down on the horizon. A few fluffy clouds caught and held the myriad of color as day turned to night and Hannah took the time to enjoy the show.

In fact, she was so caught up in nature's farewell, she didn't notice a car coming up the long dirt road until it came to a stop directly in front of the house. Stepping to the edge of the door, she peeked out the side window.

A large man with dark glasses and a slow gait made his way up the walkway. His demeanor might have seemed relaxed to the casual observer, but Hannah would never be nonchalant again. Even after Sanchez was safely locked away, she would still look at people differently. She would always be searching for hidden clues and subtle changes in body language. She was looking for them now.

The newcomer didn't appear to be in any hurry to reach the house. He stood on the edge of the porch and lit a cigarette, enjoying the same view Hannah had been savoring only moments before. The breeze caught the tendrils of smoke, swirling them about his face in an eerie dance. In the waning light she could see that he was very attractive. His dark hair was neatly combed and his jeans and shirt were clean and pressed, and his western-cut jacket was tailor-made to his muscular build. His cowboy boots shone even in the dim light and she almost made her presence known. Almost.

Just because he looked like a decent person didn't mean he wasn't on Sanchez' payroll. She knew perfectly well what caused the slight lump under his jacket. Seth had gone off to work too many mornings with the same bulge. A gun. Would he use his bullets to protect her or get her out of the way? This new cynical nature of hers was hard to accept.

He dropped the cigarette to the wooden porch and crushed it beneath his heel before turning toward the door, knocking loudly. She gave only a fleeting thought to actually opening the door. Kane would be mad enough just because she left her room. Maybe the guy would go away.

Hannah's heart pounded as he produced a key from his pocket and slid it into the dead bolt. She watched the large metal knob rotate beneath his manipulations and fought back the urge to scream when she heard the lock click, allowing him entrance.

"McCord!" His voice was deep as befitted a man of his stature. The door swung open, pinning Hannah to the wall. The man stopped just inside the door, his hand slipping inside his jacket. Moving to stand against the far wall, he peered into the back bedroom. "McCord! Where the hell are you?"

Hannah held her breath as he left the living room to investigate the kitchen. Knowing she should get the hell out of there, she quietly opened the screen door and slipped onto the front porch. *Kane, where are you?*

The sun had completely disappeared by now and a few brave stars competed with the dying light. The boards on the porch creaked slightly under her weight and she hurried down the steps onto the stone walkway. *Where could he have gone?*

She was just about to head for the garage when she sensed a presence behind her. The hair along the back of her neck prickled and she couldn't suppress a shudder as a new scent drifted to her on the lazy evening breeze. After-shave—not Kane's.

"I assume you're Hannah McCord," the man said, shifting slightly so he was in her peripheral vision.

"No," she answered quickly. Turning to face the man, she continued her lie. "My name is Dolly Matthews. Who are you?"

Replacing the gun in his shoulder holster, the man offered her a half-grin that clearly expressed his disbelief. "Well, this must be my week for Dollys. I met another Dolly Matthews just the other day. Don't suppose you're related."

Fear gripped Hannah's frantically calculating mind. This man had met Dolly. "I asked who you were."

Nodding, he reached into his jacket pocket and held out his hand. "Name's Levi Grayson. I'm with the DEA."

Hannah took the simple black leather wallet he offered and examined the name and picture inside. She really didn't put too much stock in the ID. An official-looking badge could be purchased out of a mail-order catalogue. That, along with every other piece of law-enforcement paraphernalia.

"What's this supposed to prove?" she asked, tossing

it back to him. She wouldn't feel safe until this giant had Kane's stamp of approval. Even then, his size would take some getting used to. The man had to stand well over six and a half feet and probably tipped the scales at around two hundred and fifty. That much muscle deserved an inordinate amount of respect.

"Smart lady," was his reply. Reaching into his back pocket, he produced a paperback novel. "A.L. sent this."

Taking the book, she eyed the front cover. It was the newest romance by one of her favorite authors. She allowed herself to relax *slightly*. "When did he give this to you?"

"This afternoon," he said, smiling at her caution. "Right after he assigned me to help Kane. By the way, did ya'll happen to catch the number of the truck that ran over Dreyer this morning?"

"Is he okay?" Kane had never revealed just exactly what caused him to resort to violence, but Hannah suspected it had to do with Jason's overly flirtatious attitude toward her.

"He'll live." Levi scanned the surrounding area. "Where's McCord? You shouldn't be left alone."

"I don't know where he is," she admitted, reluctant to continue the conversation. "He's probably just checking out the area."

"He still shouldn't have left—" Levi's words were cut off as a noise in the distance caught his attention. "Get in the house!"

Without bothering to argue, Hannah sped up the steps and through the front door. She dropped to her knees and crawled over to peek out the window. Levi had disappeared into the darkness.

A gnawing fear clutched at her mind. Kane was

gone. That should have been her first clue that something was wrong. What if this Levi person had bashed him over the head? She hadn't heard anything out of the ordinary just now. Maybe he was playing on her fear in order to gain her trust?

A thousand scenarios played through her mind, each more horrifying than the last. By the time Levi bounded up the front steps and into the house, Hannah had convinced herself he was the devil incarnate. Her fingers scrambled for a weapon but came up empty.

"Come on," he said, holding out his hand. "I don't know what's happened to Kane, but something's fixin' to go down and I've got to get you out of here."

"I'm not going anywhere without Kane," she insisted, her fingers finally curving around the brick they had been using as a doorstop.

"Look, lady," he growled, grabbing her arms and hoisting her to her feet. Actually she was dangling several inches off the ground as he pulled her against his chest and headed for the front door. The brick she had been holding dropped onto the toe of his boot and he glared at her for a second before thrusting open the door and charging out into the night.

Holding her under his left arm as if she were a football, Levi dashed across the front yard toward the car. As he set her on her feet in order to open the door, Hannah immediately ran in the opposite direction. "Kane!"

She could hear the man gaining on her as she hurried across the field next to the house. Her muscles tightened in anticipation of his tackle. She wasn't disappointed.

His arms snaked around her waist and they both tumbled to the ground with a thud. The force of the fall pushed the air from Hannah's lungs and she struggled for a breath. In her weakened state it was easy for him to pull her into his arms and carry her back to the car.

As soon as she caught her wind, she began to scratch at his face and kick her feet—at anything. Instead of dropping her, he tightened his hold and withstood her attack. Just as they reached the car, Hannah heard the unmistakable sound of a gunshot. Her hopes soared as she realized Kane must have heard the commotion.

Another gunshot rang through the night, followed by the resounding ping of metal on metal as the bullet struck the side of the car. Hannah resumed her struggles with her captor. "Help!"

"Shut up," he ordered, trying to force her into the car. "You're gonna get us killed."

His words only made her fight harder and she was on the edge of exhaustion when she felt his fingers tighten against the side of her neck. The strength of his hold momentarily stalled her brain's blood supply and she could feel reality slipping away. A tingling numbness forced its way through her panic and the last thing she heard before passing out was her own desperate plea. "Kane."

"Have you heard from John?" Sanchez did not like the way the McCord woman kept slipping through his fingers.

"Nothing yet," Tony admitted. *"I'll give him a few more hours."*

"I don't have to tell you how much this means to me." Sanchez saw no reason to explain himself. He was a powerful man. Tony, Bennett, Johnson. They were all just cogs in his ever-growing machine. If they could not serve him, they could be taken care of. Just like the woman.

FOURTEEN

Hannah never experienced a moment's confusion upon awakening. She was fully aware of what had happened to her. She had been kidnapped by Levi Grayson, if that was his real name, and he had used some Vulcan death grip on her. Immediate thoughts of revenge sprang to mind. Devious plans and schemes for the giant hulk of a man driving her somewhere in the darkness. She had a brief flash of the man sprawled nude across an ant bed or locked in a room with the ever-nagging Letha Thompson.

In the back of her mind she could hear her Grandmother Hanson telling her that if she acted like a lady, she would be treated like one. The disjointed thought brought a smile to her lips. *Sorry, Grandmother, but I have no intention of being a lady about this*. Taking a few moments to work the kinks out of her neck, she tried to think of some way to escape. The car was moving at a snail's pace along the dirt road, so she might be able to jump out. The pitch-black night could also act as her benefactor.

Now, what to do about Mr. Grayson. If she hadn't dropped that brick, she could hit him over the head. There was no chance she could outfight him. He would swat her like a fly.

If only she had a can of hair spray to momentarily blind him. *Think, Hannah, there has to be a way.* She thought of the movie she had seen where a man was hiding in the backseat of a woman's car. He used a scarf to wrap around her eyes. Well, it was worth a try.

Except I don't have a scarf, she thought and almost groaned out loud. There had to be something she could use to distract him so that she could jump from the car and dash out into the darkness.

Her slip!

With a minimum of movements, she managed to slide the half-slip down over her hips and legs and let it drop onto the floorboard. Through the veil of her lashes she saw him peer over the seat and she froze. He was apparently satisfied that she was still unconscious.

Keeping her head down, she shifted her body until she was crouched down behind the seat, her fingers clutching the heavy cotton of her slip. Carefully peeking over the edge of the seat, she could see the distant lights of the highway and knew she had to make her move before they reached the busy stretch of highway.

Okay, Hannah, here goes. She lifted her arms and brought the material down over the man's head, making sure she wrapped it securely around the headrest in the process. The car bounced off the road and into the sandy soil beyond. Muffled cuss words filled the air as the man struggled with both the vehicle and the slip.

Flinging open the back door, Hannah caught her breath and jumped. Even at the reduced speed, she hit the ground with a bone-jarring thud. Her knees collapsed under the sudden strain and she tumbled onto the hard-packed road. Her hair flew about her head as it came loose from the ponytail she had tied it in earlier, and she heard a distinct rip as part of her skirt tore away.

Out of the corner of her eye she noticed the car had come to a stop and the man had managed to get his door open. Swathed in her white slip he looked like an evil ghost out walking the plains. Brushing the rocks from the palms of her hands, Hannah jumped up and began stumbling in the opposite direction. She had to get as far away as she could before he managed to rip off the slip. There was no way she could outrun him, so her only hope was to get far enough away to hide.

"Hannah!" The man's voice carried to her on the night wind.

She tried to convince herself that it sounded like Kane, but she knew it was only wishful thinking on her part. She wanted so desperately for him to be there, she was imagining things.

Her hair swirled in her face and the full skirt wrapped around her legs making it impossible for her to actually run. Once she stumbled and something slithered under her hand. She bit her lip to keep from screaming. Whatever it was had to be as shocked as she was, so she just got the hell out of there before it decided on revenge.

Just when she thought she might stand a chance at getting away, she was illuminated in the beam of a flashlight. Damn, why hadn't she thought of that. Not willing to give up, she renewed her efforts to reach the highway. Maybe she could hitch a ride with a truck driver before Levi caught her.

Her blood was pounding in her ears and she pressed

her hand into her right side to quell the sharp pain she experienced with every rasping breath. Her out-of-condition body couldn't take much more of this. She was running on pure adrenalin and fear, as it was. How long could that last?

"Hannah, dammit, stop." The man was close behind her now, but she refused to give up. If he wanted her, he would have to come and get her.

She could hear his footsteps competing with hers and despite her efforts, she simply could not go any faster. Struggling to put one foot in front of the other, she pushed her body beyond its normal capacity. She stumbled, once, twice, and then he was on top of her.

The hard winter grass scraped her face as she plummeted to the ground beneath him. The awkward angle at which she fell caused her arm to be crushed under her ribs and that could only be barbed wire wrapped around her ankle.

She tried to lift him off her but simply did not have the strength. "Just shoot me and get it over with."

"I ought to, dammit." His breath was ragged as he ran his hands over her body. "Are you hurt?"

A feeble laugh made its way through the grating rasp of her breathing. "What difference does it make?"

"Hannah!" Climbing off her, he turned her onto her back and reached up to cradle her face in his hands. Brushing the wild strands of hair from her eyes, he forced her to look at him. "It's me, baby. It's me."

"Kane?" She couldn't believe her eyes. "How——"

"Don't worry about it," he ordered, brushing her lips with his. "You're safe, that's all that matters."

Of their own accord, her arms began to wrap around him. "Oh——"

"What's wrong?" Even in the dim light of the moon

he could see the pain in her face. "Where do you hurt?"

"It would be quicker to tell you where I don't hurt," she said in an attempt to dispel his concern. "I just have a few scrapes and bruises."

He ran his hands over her one more time as if to prove to himself she still had all her limbs. "That was a damned fool thing you did back there. You could have fallen under the wheel and been crushed. You could have . . ." Wrapping her tightly in his arms, he shuddered at the thought of all the things that could have happened to her.

"I'm sorry, but I thought you were trying to kidnap me." She explained about the man and the shooting. "I told him I wouldn't go without you but he refused to listen. When he heard the gunshots, he—"

"I know what he did," Kane interrupted savagely. "I could have killed him with my bare hands when I saw him touching you."

"You saw him!" Hannah tried to sit up but the pain in her side was too severe. Rather than let Kane know just how bad she hurt, she held her breath until she could find a comfortable position.

"Yeah," he whispered, disgust lacing his voice. "I saw him."

Kane had lain in Hannah's bed for a long time before giving in to his inherent need to check things out. From the corner window in Hannah's room he had spotted a reflection on a small hill just west of the farmhouse and decided to investigate. The sun was low on the horizon as he slid along the underbrush. He made a wide arc around the area until he could come up from behind.

A lone assailant had been lying in wait, his gun

trained on Hannah's window. Kane's every movement had been carefully orchestrated to give him the advantage of surprise. He was only inches away from his target when the man squeezed off a shot in the direction of the house.

Panic-filled anger fueled Kane's charge as he launched himself at the man. Years of training came into play as he did his job. The man's finger automatically tightened on the trigger one last time before Kane deftly broke his neck.

Glancing in the direction of the house, Kane had witnessed Hannah struggling with the large man. A brief flash tugged at his memory, but he ignored it as he raced toward Hannah. He had been yards away when she crumpled to the ground.

White-hot emotions tore through him as he propelled himself at this unknown enemy. Despite the difference in their size, Kane's blind fury gave him a slight edge. Bending over, he plowed into the man's midsection and heard the clatter of the gun as it fell against the car and onto the ground.

Taking advantage of the man's momentary daze, Kane grabbed him by his hair, and with a downward thrust, smashed his face into the car door. Without a sound, he collapsed at Kane's feet.

Using the toe of his boot, Kane shoved him out of the way and bent to cradle Hannah to his chest. It was already too dark to see how much damage the bastard had done, so he opened the car door and laid her on the backseat. In the glow of the car light he could easily see the rapidly coloring bruise along her neck and bile rose in his throat.

Shifting her until she was entirely in the car, Kane searched through the man's pockets until he found the keys. Despite the blood and dirt covering the man's face, Kane had another flash of recognition. He had seen this man before. But where?

He racked his brain, but he couldn't put a name with the face. Since most of his work was undercover, Kane had a suspicion that he had come upon this man during his dealings with the drug lords. If so, that meant Sanchez had discovered their whereabouts. He had to get Hannah away.

"Don't worry, baby," he whispered, climbing into the front seat. "I won't let them get you."

The car started immediately and Kane hoped he remembered the road leading back to the highway. He would drive with his lights off for security and pray they didn't end up in the bar ditch. He had already dealt with two assassins tonight; he felt sure there were more out there waiting for their chance.

Creeping along the rough terrain, Kane kept his eyes trained on the faint strip of pale dirt in front of him. The moon was just starting its ascent and was of no particular help. His fingers itched to turn on the headlights but he knew it would be folly.

Using the brakes only when he had to negotiate a sharp turn in the road, he made the painstakingly slow journey toward the paved road. Once they made the highway, he could turn on his lights and hit the gas. The highway was almost within shouting distance when he felt something slip over his head, blinding him and sending the car into a foot of loose sand.

"Damn!" he said, shaking loose from his memories and recalling the predicament they were in now. Nothing short of a tow truck would budge the car and they were miles from nowhere. Going back to the farmhouse was no longer an option.

"What?" Hannah didn't like the sound of his silence.

"How do you feel about walking?" he asked, standing up and holding out his hand.

"Walking?" she squeaked. Holding her breath, she took his hand and made it to her feet—barely. The piercing pain in her rib cage confirmed her suspicions. She had broken, or at least cracked, a rib when Kane tackled her. "Sure, no problem."

"Let's go."

Biting back a groan of agony as she managed to untangle her ankle from the spiked teeth of the barbed wire, Hannah gratefully leaned on the arm he offered. Together they began picking their way across the prairie, keeping the lights of the highway on their left. She knew if Kane realized just how bad she was hurting, he would stop.

That would put them at a greater risk and Kane's safety depended on hers. As long as she stayed out of danger, he would, too. If walking was their only chance, she'd walk.

They had been going at a slow but steady pace for more than an hour when Kane's hunch played out. Hannah was hurting a lot more than she was letting on. He had asked her more than a dozen times if she needed to rest and each time she insisted she was fine. At first he admired her guts and determination. Now, he was angered by her irresponsible courage.

"Not much farther," he said, indicating a rest area. "We ought to be able to catch a ride."

"Do you think that's a good idea?" she asked, glancing at a truck pulling into the parking area. "If we go slow, I'm sure I can make it."

"Baby," he said, shaking his head as she opened

her mouth to continue. "We've got to move fast. I don't know what happened back there, but it looks bad. Sanchez has definitely got someone feeding him information. There's no way I can draw the son of a bitch out right now, so we're on our own."

"Can't A.L. help us?"

"*If* we can get to the next town undetected. *If* I can get ahold of him without going through the agency. *If* he can maneuver without anyone finding out." He held up his fingers to emphasize each point. "Right now, it's just too risky to involve anyone else." He didn't add the last if: *if A.L. wasn't the one who sold them out.*

"But that's his job," she protested. She hadn't realized just how much she depended on the DEA doing their duty where their protection was concerned. "Don't you have some back-up plan?"

"You mean like Plan A and Plan B?"

"Does that sound so stupid?" Even though she was becoming an expert on being in danger, she still had no concept of what they really faced. "Wouldn't that be better than flying by the seat of your pants?"

"Normally, we have several contingency plans," he conceded. "But in a case like this, where someone is dirty, you have to use your guts."

"And your guts tell us to hitchhike?" She glanced over at the truck now idling beside them while its driver availed himself of the facilities.

" 'Fraid so."

It didn't take long for Kane to wield his charm on the unsuspecting driver. Hannah found herself being lifted into the cab of the truck and shifted onto the small mattress situated behind the seats. She could hear the driver rambling on about the unreliability of today's automobiles. The monotonous drone of the highway soon lulled her into a fitful sleep. She could only pray that when she woke up, she would find it was all a dream.

Kane heard her moving around behind him trying to locate a more comfortable position and flinched as he heard her moan. She was hurting and it was his fault. If only he hadn't left her alone for those few minutes. *If only*. His mind was filled with visions of what-might-have-beens.

Had he not chosen law enforcement, maybe Seth would have grown up to be a lawyer or a high school football coach. If he hadn't gone home that Thanksgiving he wouldn't have met Hannah and formed a covetous longing for his brother's wife. *If, if, if.*

Nodding occasionally at some comment good-old-David made, Kane tried to dislodge the maudlin thoughts. He had to focus on the job at hand. Whatever his feelings for Hannah, he was now solely responsible for her safety. Someone had leaked the location of the safe house and no one was above suspicion. That left him alone.

Normally, that was exactly the way he liked it. He had been called a maverick by more than one superior. Even though they didn't like it, he was much more efficient when he worked alone. Except this time. Now he had Hannah.

She shifted slightly on the bed and he heard her harsh intake of breath. In the pale glow of the interior lights, he could see the pain etched across her beautiful face and realized that her suffering hurt him more than any bullet or knife ever had.

Hell of a predicament, McCord. Stuck in the middle of nowhere with an injured woman and no backup. It was the most challenging position he had ever been in and it would take every bit of knowledge and cunning he possessed to ensure Hannah made it out alive.

When the lights of the town were only a sliver on the horizon, Kane knew what had to be done.

Tony Barlow tugged his windbreaker tighter as he made his way back to the run-down pickup parked on the dirt road. He could feel the chill seep into his bones. Or maybe it was the fact that he would have to face Sanchez with the news that the McCord woman had vanished on them again. "Hurry up, you guys. We can't afford to be seen."

The two large men following him picked up their pace despite the burden of carrying a dead comrade. They couldn't leave Johnson's body out here to be found by the feds. Sanchez would not be happy and they knew their lives depended on his satisfaction. That and the death of Hannah McCord.

FIFTEEN

"You sure you don't need a doctor to look at that nose?" A.L. handed Levi Grayson the makeshift ice pack he had formed out of a dish towel. He had found Levi stretched out on the ground when he pulled up in front of the house that morning. Kane and Hannah were both gone, and they hadn't taken a thing with them.

"It's not broken," the man assured, pressing the cloth to the proboscis in question.

A.L. shrugged his shoulders and settled onto the edge of the lounge chair opposite his fellow agent. "Feel like telling me what the hell happened out here?"

"Damned if I know." Levi eased himself back onto the couch and closed his eyes. "Why didn't you tell me the woman was a wildcat? I haven't seen anything like her since we got caught in that scuffle down in Juarez."

"Are we talkin' about the same woman here?" A.L. asked, thinking of Hannah's quiet demeanor.

"Little bitty thing," Levi raised one hand to his chest

to indicate her height. "About a hundred and twenty pounds, gold eyes, brown hair, and a temper like a cornered badger."

"Well, the physical description fits, but I can't imagine Hannah lifting her hand to anything." Jumping to his feet, A.L. began pacing across the wooden floor.

"All I can tell you is, McCord's got his hands full." Levi tossed the sopping rag onto the floor at his feet and stood up. "What's got you in such a dander?"

"You sure it was Kane that tackled you? You didn't see anyone else?"

"Yeah, pretty sure." Levi reached for the gun lying on the coffee table and slid it into his holster. Picking his jacket up off the arm of the couch, he eyed the other man. "You think there was someone else here?"

"No," A.L. answered quickly. "It's just not like McCord."

"Guess we better go look for them." Levi didn't comment that it sounded exactly like Kane McCord. For years he had gained a reputation for being a hothead. Besides, Levi could understand where Kane might have gotten the wrong idea. If he had a woman, he wouldn't like to find someone hauling her off.

"I got a bad feeling about this," A.L. admitted as they made their way to his car. "I can see why Kane would have fired a couple of shots at you, but I can't figure out why they abandoned the vehicle. It doesn't make any sense."

"Tell me something about this case that does," Levi said as he eased himself into the car.

"Not much," A.L. growled, starting the engine. "Dreyer wouldn't tell me anything and now Kane's taken Hannah and disappeared."

"They'll show up eventually," Levi assured him, his eyes scanning the flat land out his window.

"Yeah, let's just hope they're both alive and well when they do." A.L.'s normally attractive face was hardened with worry. "He could blow everything."

Levi took his eyes off the scenery to stare at his longtime friend. There was something about A.L.'s manner that bothered him. McCord was well known for both his temper and his preference for taking matters into his own hands. Even without backup, Levi had no doubts as to Kane's ability to protect the woman.

Unless there was some factor of the operation McCord didn't know about. Something A.L. had kept from him. For the first time in fifteen years, Levi wondered if he really knew the man sitting next to him.

Kane unlocked the motel door with one hand while balancing two cups of coffee and a plate with the other. He waited for Hannah to step across the threshold and switch on the lights. "This place looks better in the dark."

"Don't worry about it," Hannah said, heading for the bathroom. "It's got a bed and a bathtub."

The dim light of one lone lamp fought against the bleak room. Kane kicked the door shut with his foot. The damned room was bad enough without any light showing off its numerous flaws. Still, it was exactly the type of place he had been looking for—slightly off the main road with a half-drunk manager. "You doin' okay in there?"

A tortured silence filled the room before she answered. "No."

Not bothering to knock, Kane swung open the door. "What's wrong—" His sentence was cut off by the sharp intake of his breath as he witnessed the bruise running just under the delicate white lace of her bra. "Why didn't you tell me?"

"I didn't know it was this bad," she admitted, still trying to remove her sweater. "I think I cracked a rib."

"You're damned lucky you didn't break your neck," he growled. With infinite tenderness, Kane lifted the sweater over her head. "I want you to soak in a hot tub and then I'm going to look at those ribs."

"You won't get any arguments from me."

"That'll be the day." Once the tub was full of steamy water, Kane helped her remove the rest of her clothes and eased her into the tub. "I'll come help you out in a little while."

"I can stand up by myself," she protested.

"I didn't say you couldn't," he said quietly. They both knew there was no way she could get out of the tub by herself. "I was just being a gentleman."

"That'll be the day." She threw his words back at him as he shut the door. Her skin was tingling both from the temperature of the water and the heated look Kane had cast at her naked body before leaving. In spite of the circumstances and her injuries, she felt a now-familiar longing.

What's the matter with me? she thought, sliding the tiny bar of soap between her palms until a frothy lather ran down her arms. *I've got people trying to kill me. I'm hiding out in some roach-infested motel room. My ribs are cracked and I haven't eaten in over twenty-four hours. How can I even think about making love?*

She was still thinking about it when he opened the door thirty minutes later. "Ready?"

Thinking he had read her mind, she blushed and tried

to cover herself with the washcloth. "You don't need to help me."

"Hannah, just shut up." Draping one of the thin, grayish towels over his arm, Kane leaned over and lifted Hannah against his chest. The feel of her slick, wet body in his arms caused the very physical reaction he had been trying to avoid for the last half hour. He had done everything but pour ice down the front of his jeans in order to maintain the control he desperately needed. "Dry off."

"Don't be such a grouch." Taking the towel, Hannah blotted at the moisture covering her skin. "I'm fine now. You can leave."

"Great." Stalking from the room, Kane mumbled something about filling the ice bucket and she heard the door slam shut. He immediately unlocked it and stepped back inside. "Keep this door locked while I'm gone."

"Yes, sir." Hannah would have saluted if her ribs would have allowed.

"I mean it," he ordered, shaking the ice bucket in her direction.

"I'm sorry," she said quietly. "You know best."

"Damned right I do," he ground out, still shaken by the sight of her standing there wrapped in what barely passed for a towel. "But you're gonna have to do exactly what I tell you. *Exactly*."

"I always do," she protested.

"What a crock!" Flinging his arm at the surroundings, he returned his gaze to her. "If you had listened to me, we wouldn't be in this mess."

"That's not fair—" Hannah stopped when she realized she was talking to thin air. It wasn't that she didn't *try* to do what he told her to, but it was hard. She had every confidence in Kane's abilities, but she had also learned not to blindly follow the rules.

All her life she had obeyed the dictates of society without question. As a little girl she played with dolls and had tea parties instead of climbing trees and dissecting grasshoppers. In school she maintained a straight-A average and only dated nice, respectable young men, even though she was secretly attracted to the boys that had an air of danger about them. She would never have dreamed of marrying a man her parents didn't approve of or choosing a career that wasn't considered proper.

During her marriage she allowed Seth to take care of everything from paying the bills to deciding where they would live. Just as her father had been, Seth was the undisputed head of the household. So she allowed him to plot the course of their lives without so much as voicing her opinion. She had truly believed, if she played by the rules, nothing bad would happen. She had been wrong.

Hannah knew there wasn't anything she could have done to prevent Seth's murder. Being a cop wasn't just his job, it was part of who he was. She would never have dreamed of asking him to give it up. She had always known the risks.

What she hadn't known was how lost she would be without him. She had no idea of their financial situation or how to handle the mundane things like changing the oil in the car. Everything had been in Seth's name. It was like Hannah Elizabeth Hanson McCord had never lived.

And she hadn't. She merely existed on the periphery of life—never making waves or causing trouble. When Grandma Hanson offered her the farm, it was like being born again. For the first time in her life, Hannah had to depend on herself and her own judgment. She had learned the hard way that rules were indeed made to be broken.

Hannah hurriedly washed out her underthings in the bathroom sink and flung them across the towel rod. Kane was taking a long time getting the ice but she knew she wouldn't be able to sleep until he returned.

Stretching out on the lumpy mattress, Hannah pulled the thin blanket over her nude body and waited. As soon as he got back, they would share the simple breakfast Kane had managed to round up while checking in. *Hurry up, Kane, I want to eat and go to sleep.* Her body relaxed into the soft mattress and her eyes refused to stay open. Maybe she would just rest them for a few minutes.

She never heard Kane's key in the door. The coffee was ice cold and the cinnamon rolls were rock hard by the time she opened her eyes.

"Good grief!" she exclaimed, rubbing her eyes. "What happened to you?"

"Just a little disguise to throw them off," he explained the change in his appearance. Nothing drastic— a haircut and shave—but it might be enough. He reached over and fingered the mass of brown hair spilling over her shoulder. "We're gonna have to do something about you, too."

"Do you have any scissors?"

If Kane was surprised by her attitude, he didn't show it. Instead, he reached into one of the bags he was holding and pulled out a pair of scissors and one of those do-it-yourself permanents. Hannah took a few moments to shower while he was constructing a make-shift beauty salon.

"I don't suppose you thought of lunch?" she asked,

stepping into the room with only a towel wrapped around her.

"You suppose wrong," he said and produced a large bag bearing the logo of a familiar fast-food restaurant. "Are you sure you don't mind cutting your hair?"

"No," she promised, digging into the bag and withdrawing a hamburger. "I've been thinking about it for a while."

They both made short work of the meal and Hannah situated herself on one of the rickety chairs by the small table. Kane unwrapped a brand-new comb and brush and began the task of untangling Hannah's still-wet hair.

"We could buy a wig," he suggested, the scissors poised over the section of hair she had instructed him to cut.

"Just do it."

Grimacing, Kane positioned the scissors, and with a quick snip, the long strand of hair fell to the floor at his feet. With Hannah guiding him through the process, he managed to fashion a fairly decent shoulder-length bob. "Hey, that's not half bad."

Swiveling around, Hannah stared at herself in the mirror over the scarred dresser. The ends were slightly jagged and one side was just a tad shorter than the other, but all in all he had done a decent job. The permanent would help to even things up anyway.

Kane insisted on reading the instructions for the perm at least four times before he felt comfortable with the rolling process. "Now what?"

"This goes on first," she said, holding up the bottle of waving solution. She positioned three towels around her neck and held a washrag over her face. "Just snip off the tip and squirt it on every curl."

"Damn, this stuff stinks," he complained once the process was completed. "You mean, women do this to themselves all the time?"

"You men would be surprised at what we do for you." Smiling at his look of disbelief, Hannah recalled how many times Seth had been equally shocked. Plucking eyebrows, curling eyelashes, bikini waxes, and mud packs. They all liked to think women were just naturally perfect.

By the time they finished the neutralizing, Hannah's uneven bob was a full, wavy mass of curls. She was already in love with her new look. "I should have done this years ago," she called from the bathroom where she stood in front of the mirror, fluffing her newly acquired bangs.

"Let me see." Kane came to join her in the small confines of the room. He stood in the doorway, not saying a word.

Hannah took his silence for disapproval and felt a pang of disappointment. She had hoped he would be just as thrilled with her new hairstyle. "It'll grow back."

"No," he whispered, reaching up to finger one of the curls framing her face. "It's perfect. You look like an angel."

"Really?"

"Yeah," he said, moving to sit on the edge of the sink. He pulled her into the space between his legs and held her face with his hands. "My angel."

Forgetting her injuries and the thin towel wrapped around her, Hannah leaned into his embrace. He buried his face into her hair seeking the delicate skin behind her ear. His lips moved over her flesh, sending shivers of excitement coursing through her. "Kane."

"Hannah," he said, his voice husky with need. "We don't have any business doing this right now."

"I know," she agreed, shifting in his arms to allow his questing fingers better access to the secrets beneath the terry cloth.

Leaning back on the sink, he slipped his fingers beneath the top of the towel and eased it away. Ever cautious of her ribs, he caressed the delicate underside of her breast. She jerked in his arms. "We should stop."

"Okay." Instead of pulling back, she slanted her body across his.

It took them a second to realize that the loud crack they heard was the sound of the sink coming loose from the wall.

"What the hell?" Kane jumped up off the sink, taking Hannah with him. Their combined weight had broken the seal between the porcelain sink and the tile on the wall. Luckily, the pipes held. "Talk about an omen."

Even though her body protested, her mind saw the humor in the situation. "We almost got a cold shower the hard way."

"It sure put a *damper* on things," he joked, checking the stability of the sink. "I think it'll hold."

"Actually, it looks better this way," she said, indicating the sagging bed, off-center mirror, and drooping drapes. "Now it matches the rest of the room."

"You deserve better than this," he said, his good humor gone. He reached up to pluck her underwear from the towel rod. "I'll get your clothes."

So much for romance, she thought, slipping into her panties. She didn't quite understand why Kane was convinced that she was some hothouse flower who couldn't tolerate the realities of life. Not only had she dealt with Seth's murder, but she had managed to endure the hardships of the last few weeks without falling apart. What would it take for him to realize that she was a strong woman, capable of surviving in his world.

"Here, I hope these are the right size," he said, shoving a pair of jeans and soft pink sweater at her. "I wasn't sure if you'd like the color."

"It's beautiful," she assured. The jeans were a soft, stone-washed blue that looked like they had been worn often. The soft turtleneck sweater easily covered the bruise on the side of her neck. If she only had a little mascara and some lipstick, she would look like a normal person.

Kane was standing in front of the window staring at the passing cars when she entered the room. His appearance was still a shock to her. His hair had been trimmed close on the sides and in back, leaving only partial fullness on top. If anything, the shortness only accentuated the gray.

What she missed the most, though, was his mustache. That thick brush of black and gray had somehow personified him, giving him a rakish, devil-may-care aura that was incredibly sexy. Now, he looked so *proper*. She missed her rogue.

"What are you looking for?"

He shrugged his shoulders without turning around. There was an edginess in his manner, a need for action that made itself known in every nuance of his handsome features. "I have to go out for a while, but I hate to leave you alone."

"Can't I go with you?" She came to stand beside him but didn't reach out to touch him. "I'll be good."

"Sure you will," he said, his voice full of sarcasm.

"No, I have to go alone." He glanced at her and saw the uncertainty written across her face. "Listen, Hannah, I can't trust *anyone* but you right now. I need to know I can depend on you."

"I'll be okay," she promised. Her fingers lightly caressed the muscles of his arm before she leaned into him. "You do whatever it is you need to do."

"Can you use a gun?" he asked, lifting his foot onto the chair situated in front of them. "I mean, really use it, not just hold it."

"Yes, I can use one." She watched him lift the hem of his jeans to reveal a small silver pistol.

"This is a—"

"AMT .380," she said, taking the gun from him. "Seth had one just like it."

Kane was relieved to see that she did indeed know her way around firearms. Her life could very well depend on her ability to aim and fire the semiautomatic pistol at an enemy. Actually shooting someone was the hardest thing he had ever had to do; he suspected it would be damned near impossible for Hannah. "You may have to use it."

"I know." Her voice was barely audible as she turned the gun over in her palm, testing its weight. Raising her eyes to his, she nodded. "I can if I have to."

"I shouldn't be gone more than an hour," he said, taking her hand in his and leading her to the door. "I'm going to try and locate some sort of transportation to Albuquerque. I have a few favors I can call in. I want you to stay in this room until I get back." He hesitated, his hand on the doorknob. "If I don't come back—"

"You'll be back." She refused to think otherwise.

"Hannah." He opened the door, but instead of stepping out into the afternoon sun, he turned back to pull her into his arms. There was a desperation in his kiss that scared her. It was as if he never expected to hold her again.

SIXTEEN

"Kane, where are you?" she asked the night. It was already twenty minutes past eight but she refused to give up just yet. She would wait another five minutes before she called Eli. Or maybe ten.

Her jaw muscles ached from gritting her teeth in frustration. He said an hour. That had been three hours ago. How long could it take to check out the bus schedule? She had to face the fact that something or someone was keeping him from coming back to her.

What would she do if he never returned? Would calling Eli put him at risk? *Of course it will, you idiot.* Everything about this situation was dangerous. Especially if one of the DEA agents was working with Sanchez.

She still had a hard time accepting Kane's suspicions about Jason and A.L. Jason was nothing more than an aging Lothario who enjoyed flirting with any woman in sight. She knew the fact that she and Kane were basically a couple only added to Jason's warped idea of entertainment. He might be irritating but he wasn't crooked.

As for A.L., she couldn't believe he would ever do anything to hurt her. Or Kane. There was a tangible closeness between the two men that was obvious to even the most casual observer. No, it would take something really tragic before A.L. would turn against them.

By nine o'clock she knew there was no choice. She reached for the ancient black phone on the nightstand between the beds and dialed the Hanson County Sheriff's Office. With each rotation of the dial, her heart beat faster. "Hello, Texetta."

A shrill whistle blasted Hannah's eardrum and she jerked the phone from her ear. Another long toot followed the first and she almost hung up.

"Hannah, honey, is that you?" Texetta's voice was urgent on the other end.

"Texetta, what's wrong? What was that noise? Is Eli there?" The receiver slipped in her palm and she wiped her hand on the leg of her jeans.

"Honey, I don't know where he is," Texetta offered. "He never showed up for work this mornin' and his bed hasn't been slept in. You know how messy he is, but Dolly was over there yesterday and cleaned up that rat's nest he lives in. She did a good job, too, I can tell you that. I was a little surprised by this thing between the two of them, but I think Dolly's good for him. She's—"

"Texetta!" Hannah interrupted. "Have you called Dolly?"

"Well, of course I have. Do you think I'm an idiot?"

"Sorry, I'm just upset," Hannah apologized and calmed her voice. "Tell me why you think something is wrong?"

"Well, those uppity federal guys have been crawlin' all over this place for the last week." Texetta lowered her voice to a whisper before continuing. "I wouldn't be a bit surprised to find out this phone is bugged. That's why I whistled into the receiver when I picked it up. I saw that in a movie one time."

"Never mind that." Hannah tried to think of where Eli might have gone. It wasn't like him at all to go off without telling someone where he could be located. "Are any of those federal guys still hanging around?"

"Not a one," Texetta said. "I think that's pretty coincidental. They disappeared the same time as Eli. I bet they took him off somewhere."

"Oh, Texetta, I don't think so," Hannah said, but her mind was frantic. What if Kane had been right and there was a leak in the agency? What if that person had Eli right now? What if he had Kane?

"Listen here, missy, you didn't see 'em." Texetta raised her voice as if she expected every word to be recorded. "They all had shifty eyes. And not a one of them liked my blueberry cobbler."

Some people thought you could tell the good guys from the bad by the color of their Stetson. For Texetta, it was her blueberry cobbler. If a man went back for seconds, he had to be on the straight and narrow. The problem was her cooking. She was the world's worst cook and it took a cast-iron stomach to handle more than a small portion of the deadly pastry.

"Texetta, let's forget your cobbler for a minute," Hannah coaxed, desperate to find Eli. "When was the last time you talked to him?"

"It was right before that A.L. guy left last night. I was closing up shop, waiting for Maybelle to take over the dispatching." Texetta paused a moment as if collecting her thoughts. "That boy came in and marched right into Eli's office. I couldn't hear what was goin' on because he closed the door."

Hannah knew that to Texetta, a closed door was an open invitation to snoop. She liked to imagine herself the Western version of Miss Marple. "Did you hear anything?"

"Just a little," the older woman admitted. "That A.L. was asking Eli if he had heard from you because you were missin'. When Eli got upset, A.L. told him to leave it to the experts. Just who does he think he is? Why, Eli Gunn is the best lawman I've ever seen. He's not like most sheriffs. He's been to all those schools and had plenty of trainin'—"

"Texetta!" Hannah interrupted again. "I know Eli is the best. That's why I need to find him."

"Honey, like I told that big feller that came in about an hour ago, I don't have any idea."

Hannah's mind was instantly on the alert. "What fellow was that?"

"Another one of those agents. But he was a good one," she assured. "Ate three helpin's of cobbler."

"What was his name?" Hannah was running out of time and patience.

"Levi somethin'," Texetta said. "Do you suppose he was named for the jeans or the Bible?"

Levi Grayson. What did he want with Eli? "What did he need?"

"Just asked to see the sheriff. When I told him Eli had been out of the office all day and I didn't have a gnat's worth of idea where he was, he took out of here like a scalded cat."

Hannah could hear Texetta talking to someone in the office. "Hannah, here, Dolly wants to talk to you."

"Hannah?" Dolly's voice held a breathy quality that suggested a brisk trot. "Are you okay? Have you heard from Eli?"

"I'm fine," Hannah assured her and explained why she and Kane had left the safe house. "But I haven't heard from Eli. That's why I was calling."

"Damn, I just knew he was somewhere with you and Kane." Dolly mumbled something to Texetta before continuing her conversation. "Listen, Hannah, something is going on around here. Those DEA guys were running around like chickens with their heads cut off and once Eli found out you guys were missing, he just about came unglued."

"I'm fine, but I don't know about—"

"Don't say anything important, Hannah," Dolly cautioned. "They've got the whole place bugged in case Sanchez calls. Do you think they're running a trace now?"

"How am I supposed to know?" Hannah asked in desperation. "I'm an elementary-music teacher. I don't know any more about this stuff than you do. If TV is anything to go by, I imagine they'll be knocking on the door in a few minutes."

"You better get out of there," Dolly squealed, her panic easily transmitted across the lines. "Go to a phone booth and call back."

"Okay." Hannah hung up and took a minute to gather her thoughts. If what Dolly and Texetta suspected was true and the phone lines were tapped, they could easily have traced the call to the motel.

There was a convenience store about a block away. She could use the phone. Tucking the gun into the back of her pants, she pulled the sweater down over it and opened the door. "Shoot, I don't have a key."

Recalling something she had seen on TV, she grabbed one of the bandages from the box Kane had purchased earlier and applied it to the doorjamb. The sticky tape held to the metal and prevented the lock from sliding into the slot. The door opened easily.

She tried to concentrate on everything that was happening around her. In the last few days she had developed a habit of being observant. Everyone was a potential enemy and each avenue a possible escape.

The bright lights of the convenience store lit her way down the darkened alley from the motel. A few stray cats were scavenging in a large red dumpster and Hannah's presence startled them. Her heart ached for the homeless animals and she thought of Diogee. Was he doing better? Did he miss her as much as she missed him?

The phones were attached to the far south wall but neither one was in working order. Glancing around, Hannah spotted a nightclub a couple of blocks away. As she made her way to the bar, she was grateful for the partial darkness of the area.

The bar was throbbing with the beat of a slow country and western song and she received several appreciative glances as she made her way from the front door to the phone on the back wall. Ignoring the suggestive smirks of a few overindulging men, Hannah concentrated on digging out the change that had been left over after she purchased dinner.

"Texetta, it's me."

"How are you, *Barbara Ann*?" Texetta asked, emphasizing the name.

"I'm doin' fine." Hannah consciously dipped her voice an octave. Was Texetta just being cautious or had something happened in the last few minutes to warrant the additional precaution. "Can I speak to the sheriff?"

"He's not here right now," Texetta spoke softly and Hannah could hear a man's voice in the background. "Can you call back tomorrow?"

"I'll do that." Hannah hung up the phone. The shivers that shook her had nothing to do with the chilly November night. Someone was there. Had her phone call put Dolly and Texetta in greater danger?

Striding purposefully out of the smoke-filled bar, Hannah carefully made her way back to the motel. She noticed a brown four door sedan parked across the street. It hadn't been there earlier, and instead of heading for the motel, she turned into a diner.

Her hand was on the door when a large arm slid around her waist and she was hauled up against a very male chest. Reacting on gut instinct, she opened her lips to scream just as her assailant's hand covered her mouth. "Hush, Hannah, it's me."

"Mumphon?" she asked, through his tightly clenched fingers. Turning her head to the side, she caught a glimpse of a perfectly coiffed blond head

"Promise you won't scream?"

Hannah nodded her head and took a deep breath as soon as he removed his hand. "You almost suffocated me, Jason. What's going on here?"

"I don't have any idea," he admitted, leading her toward the sedan she had noticed earlier. "I got a call from Kane telling me to pick you up here. I almost didn't recognize you with your new haircut."

Reaching up to finger the back of her hair, Hannah tried to figure out what was going on. "Why did he call *you?*"

Jason opened the car door and shoved her into the

seat before loping around to the other side. Within seconds, he had slid the key into the ignition and was pulling out of the parking lot. "Beats the heck out of me. About fifteen minutes ago, I pick up the phone and there he was, sending me out here. I gotta tell you I was shocked as hell to hear from him after the other day, but when it comes down to it, I guess we guys have to stick together."

"Jason, I don't like this," Hannah said. She was amazed at how quickly he had gotten her into the car without giving her time to protest his actions. Staring out the window, she tried to make sense of Jason's erratic driving. He was turning at almost every corner and continued to check the rearview mirror. "I think you better take me back."

"Look . . ." Jason's eyes never left the road as he reached over to grab her hand. "I know this seems like a nightmare to you, but it will all be over soon. I found out today that they managed to move the trial up to Monday instead of Wednesday."

"How do you know?" she asked as the brightly lit residential section gave way to a darker, less populated, industrial district. "Where are we going?"

"I have a friend who works at the courthouse." Jason squeezed her hand. "Gloria told me this afternoon that the judge is moving up the docket."

"Gloria?" The name was familiar to her. "Wasn't she the one you called from the safe house?"

Releasing her hand, Jason gripped the steering wheel firmly as he slowed the car for another turn. "Yeah. I want to apologize for that. Kane was right to flip out. I had no business calling her from there, but I've only been seeing her a few weeks and, well, you know how it is at the beginning." He slowed for a stoplight and then turned right. "I was afraid someone else would come along while I was off babysitting you."

Hannah was surprised at the sincerity in Jason's voice. Either his apology was heartfelt or he was a number-one con man. He hadn't answered her second question, though, and she had the impression he had no intention of doing so. "Jason, either you tell me where we are going or I'm getting out."

With lightning reflexes, Jason grabbed her arm and yanked her across the seat next to him. "Don't be a fool. I'm not going to hurt you. I'm just taking you to meet Kane so the two of you can get out of town."

Hannah searched his profile for some hint of the truth. Was he really going to deliver her to Kane? Or someone else? She mentally shook her head at the notion of Jason turning her over to Sanchez. Even clasped to his side, traveling down a deserted street in the dead of night, Hannah could not picture Jason being so cruel. "Can you at least tell me what's been going on the last twenty-four hours?"

Jason seemed to sense her trust and he loosened his hold on her as he pulled the car into the parking lot of what used to be a natural-gas plant. Dead grass and weeds were sprouting from the large cracks in the pavement and the streetlamp on the corner was out. All in all, it was the last place on earth she would have chosen to meet Kane.

"I don't have a clue, Hannah," Jason admitted as he turned off the headlights and killed the engine. "I've been in a hotel room nursing a few pretty bad bruises since yesterday morning." He slid out his side of the car and pulled her along with him. "I was planning on sending out for pizza and a bottle of whiskey when A.L. called and told me to go get you."

"I thought you said Kane called you." Tugging out of his grasp, Hannah pressed herself against the car, refusing to go with him. The small of her back made contact with the door, causing the gun resting in her waistband to press painfully into her skin. She grabbed for the weapon, intending to hold it on Jason until he told her the truth, but his years of experience and training easily outmaneuvered her feeble efforts. "Give that to me."

"Hannah, I might be stupid, but I'm not suicidal." He slid the pistol into his jacket pocket and held out his hand to her. "Come on, it isn't safe for you to be out here in the open. A.L. and Levi should be here soon."

"Levi?" Hannah stuck her hands behind her back and grabbed the door handle for support, but Jason easily overpowered her and led her into the abandoned building. Even after years of disuse, the dilapidated structure still held the unmistakable odor of sour gas and oil. Hannah's foot slipped on a slick spot in the floor and she was grateful for Jason's quick reflexes. "You mean he really is an agent?"

"Hell, yes, he's an agent." Jason seemed surprised at her question. He took them deeper into the dark recesses of the plant, sidestepping broken pipes and other debris. His tone seemed ominous in the cavernlike section of the interior. "In my opinion, he's the best there is. When did you meet him?"

"I guess he was supposed to be your replacement. He and Kane had a disagreement," Hannah whispered, uneasy at how her voice carried. A streetlight from the alley barely managed to glimmer through the filthy windows lining the upper edge of the back wall.

Raising his hand to finger his still-swollen upper lip,

Jason grinned. "Kane does seem to be having a lot of those lately. I take it *that's* why you and McCord took off on your own."

Hannah nodded. She had to think of some way to convince Jason to take her back to the motel. Kane was surely there by now and he would be frantic. "Jason, please take me to Kane. He'll be worried."

Jason seemed to be debating her request. Finally he shook his head. "Tell you what I'll do. After I've delivered you safely into A.L.'s hands, I'll go back to the motel and tell McCord what happened. He won't like it, but at least he'll know you're safe."

"You can't leave me with A.L.," Hannah cried as he reached out and grabbed her arm. The echo of the plant only intensified her anguish. "Kane thinks there's a leak in the agency somewhere. What if it's A.L.? Or Levi?"

"A leak?" Jason's hand dropped, and even in the pale light she could see his astonishment. "Why does he suspect there's a leak?"

"Because of the man that tried to shoot me back at the safe house." Hannah took a few minutes to explain all that had transpired since Kane and Jason's fight almost two days ago. "Kane said only a few people at the agency knew the exact location. I know he doesn't want to believe it's A.L., but it has to be somebody."

Jason didn't answer her. In the silence, Hannah began to listen to the sounds of the night. The far-off rumble of the interstate traffic, the occasional scurry of a night creature upset at having its home invaded, the horrifying whisper of her own thoughts. She was just about to break the silence when Jason suddenly grabbed her arm and began pulling her back toward the front of the plant. "Jason? What's wrong?"

"I've got to get you out of here," he said almost to himself. "Damn!"

"Jason, please, tell me what's wrong." Hannah could feel the brittle edge of hysteria threatening to rip away any shred of control she maintained.

Stepping quickly toward the west side of the building, Jason shoved her behind several large pieces of metal sheeting leaning against the wall. "I've got to check things out. I'll be back."

"Jason, wait—" But he was already slipping through the darkness. Wrapping her arms around her waist, Hannah snuggled between the relative safety of heavily rusted metal and the deteriorating wall. *What a crummy place to die.* The thought came before she had time to stop it.

Hannah was too tired and too worried to give herself a pep talk. At this point she was more than willing to admit she wanted nothing more than for Kane to show up on his white horse and carry her off to safety. She didn't want to be an independent, self-sufficient wonder woman. She wanted her man.

How had things gotten so messed up? One minute she had Kane in her arms and the next she was fighting a modern-day version of Paul Bunyan before heading off to fight the bad guys alone. One minute she believed in fairy tales and happily-ever-afters and the next she was praying Sanchez didn't have a penchant for killing people slowly. If she ever got off this nightmarish roller coaster, she was going back to Hanson, where Letha Thompson was the meanest person she had to face.

Hannah knew her life would be incredibly empty without Kane, but she'd had all the Adventures in Narcoticsland she could handle. She was a normal person. A person who went to church on Sunday, stopped at crosswalks, and paid her taxes. Surely putting one slimy, murdering drug dealer behind bars was all anyone could ask of her. No one would expect her to sit at home wondering if Kane would meet the same fate as his brother. Even Kane wouldn't expect that of her. Just like she didn't expect him to give up his life to become a gentleman farmer in Hanson County, New Mexico.

So much for that second chance.

"Hannah!" Jason's hoarse whisper startled her out of her private pity party. Pulling her from behind the metal, he grabbed her hand and led her toward the side door of the building.

"What's happening?" Following him into the chilly night, Hannah pressed herself against the wall for support.

He reached into his pocket and handed her gun back to her. "I'm sorry, Hannah. So damned sorry."

Hannah could hear the terrifying sounds of running feet and whispered orders coming around the corner of the building. "Is it A.L.? Was he the leak?"

Without warning, Jason pulled her into his embrace. "No, I'm the damned leak. Looks like my big mouth got me in the end. I only hope A.L. gets here in time to save you."

"Jason, stop it." She bit back the urge to scream. "I don't understand."

"Gloria!" He spat the name into the night. Shaking Hannah's shoulders, he continued. "The only people who knew about the safe house were A.L., Hooper, and me. I couldn't resist asking Gloria to meet me. I even called her tonight and told her that I would be free after I delivered you to A.L. The bitch must be on the take."

"Dear Lord," Hannah whispered as his meaning became clear. "Then that's Sanchez out there."

"Listen." He was suddenly all business. "I can hold them off until A.L. shows up. But not if I've got to keep you covered. You've got to find a place to hide."

"I can help," she argued, believing in the old adage about safety in numbers. "I know how to shoot this."

"I hope like hell you don't have to," was his only reply. His lips came down on hers in a brief good-luck kiss and he pushed her toward the metal maze of the plant.

Stumbling over fallen boards and wires, Hannah hurried away from the resumed sounds of the fight. Hopefully someone had already heard the noise and put in a call to 911. With any luck the entire area would soon be swarming with cops.

Running her hands along the side of the small, square building in front of her, she hoped for a door handle. Instead she found a set of stairs leading up to the top of the three-story structure. The rapid fire of gunshots growing closer made her decision for her. Clasping her pistol in one hand and the rusty handrail in the other, she began the treacherous climb to what she hoped was safety.

SEVENTEEN

Kane wasn't exactly sure how, but he knew Hannah was gone before he even reached the motel. Blame it on ESP or gut instinct, but he knew. Steering the rattletrap of a car he had managed to secure into the parking lot of a bar across the street, he forced his emotions to the back of his mind.

He took a few deep breaths and began drawing on his years of experience to guide him. There were only two reasons for Hannah not staying in the room. One, she left of her own accord. Two, she was forced. Either way, it threw a monkey wrench into his carefully-detailed plans.

According to the schedule he had mapped out, they should be on their way to Ruidoso within the hour. Anything later than that would set off a series of missed connections that wouldn't be easily corrected. Hitting the steering wheel with the palm of his hand, he snatched the keys from the ignition and left the vehicle. A glance at the rusted fender and dented hood assured him there was no need to lock the doors.

He was in the middle of crossing the street when he noticed the door to his motel room open. Breaking into a jog, he prayed his instincts were wrong and Hannah's face would appear in the dim light. Just before the interior lights were snapped out, he caught a glimpse of a very familiar face. A.L.

Tamping down a sudden surge of fear-charged adrenaline, Kane quickly made his way around the motel diner and into the back alley. Just as he came upon the back side of the row of rooms, he witnessed another man striding across the parking lot toward A.L. It was the man from the safe house. The one who had been taking off with Hannah.

For years Kane had made his way by blending into the woodwork. He used his abilities now as he crept closer to the pair. When he crouched down behind the right rear tire of a minivan, he was able to hear bits and pieces of their conversation.

"Are you sure you told him to wait for us here?" the large man asked, scanning the parking lot. Kane knelt on the asphalt to minimize the chance of being spotted.

"I'm positive," A.L. assured him. Kane could hear the agitation in his old friend's voice. Something had gone wrong and he only hoped it wouldn't place Hannah in greater danger. "After we traced the call, I contacted him and told him about the transfer. He said he would meet us here and we could confront them together. If they left." He indicated the room with a nod of his head. "They didn't take anything with them. Of course that could be to throw us off."

"Look, A.L., McCord is more than capable of taking care of the woman. I'll bet dollars to donuts, they took off before Dreyer even got here."

"Then where is Dreyer?" A.L. asked, looking around the parking lot one more time.

Kane had heard enough. It was time to make his presence known. "That's what I'd like to know."

"McCord."

"Kane." A.L. automatically took a step but pulled up short when he saw the weapon in Kane's hands. "What's going on, man?"

"I'll ask the questions," Kane said, motioning with the barrel of his gun. "Who's he?"

A.L. glanced over his shoulder at the big man defending his back. "You've met Levi Grayson before. He worked on the Palomino case back in '85."

So that was where he had seen the man. The Palomino case had been one of the few complete successes for the DEA. It had been a major undertaking involving hundreds of agents and other law-enforcement personnel. Kane had been in deep cover for more than a year.

"After our encounter yesterday I realized you must have associated me with my undercover persona. Sorry about that." Levi stepped forward in spite of the gun pointed at his midsection and held out his hand.

Kane met the man's open stare and slid the gun into his pocket before accepting the peace offering. "I couldn't afford to take any chances. Especially after I'd just popped one of Sanchez's men."

"What?" both of the agents asked in unison.

Kane explained about his reasons for leaving Hannah alone in the house and the ensuing battle on the hill. "It was the hit man who fired those shots, not me."

A.L. ran a shaky hand over his face. "There's a leak."

"Yeah," Kane said. Striding toward the motel room,

he dug his key out of his pocket and opened the door. "That's why I'm worried."

"At least you've got Hannah tucked away," Levi said, shutting the door behind them.

"No," Kane admitted as he picked up the soft green sweater Hannah had worn. "I left her here a few hours ago. I don't know where she is."

A.L. spent the next few minutes on the phone, but to no avail. Dreyer wasn't at his hotel room and no one knew where to reach him. "I'll bet he took her to the transfer site."

"That stupid son of a bitch." Levi actually voiced the other men's opinion of their fellow agent. By not following orders, Jason had put Hannah in greater danger. Possibly even dooming their plans to get her to safety.

"Let's go." Kane slid his gun out of his pocket and double checked his ammunition. He hoped they would find Jason and Hannah calmly waiting for them at the abandoned plant A.L. had described as the transfer site. If not, they would have to be ready.

Hannah felt the stairs wobble with each careful step and held her breath. She was already more than halfway up the zigzag ladder leading to the top of the building. If she could just make it without slipping and plummeting to the ground, she might stand a chance.

The sounds of the fight were sporadic. An eternal silence followed by a brief period of gunfire. As long as the shots still rang out, she had hope. It was only during those quiet times that she had a clear mental image of Jason lying dead in a pool of his own blood.

The top was almost within her reach when she heard angry voices directly below her. Pressing her back against the outer wall, she dared to glance down. Two men were arguing, their voices raised, arms gesturing wildly in the direction Jason had run. They apparently came to some sort of agreement, because they took off in separate directions leaving her still plastered to the side of the building.

Checking the back of her waistband for the pistol, Hannah quickly climbed the remaining stairs and eased herself onto the wooden roof. The ancient boards creaked under the sudden strain of her weight. The slight noise sounded like an explosion to her ears. Holding her breath, she half expected to find one of the men scurrying up the ladder after her.

After a few seconds, she tried another step. The moon was bright enough for her to make out clearly three large round encasements on the roof. Each tube stood well over her head and she carefully made her way around the first one. An abrupt spurt of gunfire caused her to drop to her knees and huddle next to the fiberglass cylinder.

The faint sound of voices calling her name was carried to her on the evening breeze and her heart froze as she realized there would be no more gunshots. The voices held a distinct Spanish accent. Jason must be dead and now they were looking for her.

Crawling on her hands and knees, she headed for the edge of the tower. If she could locate them it would help her maintain her advantage. Just before she reached the ledge of the roof, her fingers slid over a metal chain. Thinking the chain might come in handy, Hannah tugged on the cold metal. The night was filled with the sound of popping wood and creaking metal as a trapdoor opened next to her. There was no way the men on the ground hadn't heard. Still, she reasoned, they wouldn't be able to determine her exact location.

As she peered into the dark void of the building, she caught a faint glimmer of metal. It stood to reason that the trap door would lead to an inner section. If so, there would have to be more stairs leading down.

Hannah sat on the roof and lowered her legs into the opening. With careful movements, she managed to locate a simple rung ladder. Her hands grasped the rough wood and, for a second, she debated the wisdom of her actions. The ladder had to be several years old and it might not withstand her weight. She could be rushing into a predicament equally as dangerous as that on the ground. If the ladder broke, she would fall and no one would ever find her in this place.

The irony of her situation struck her as the sound of angry male voices overrode her fears and she lowered herself down into the belly of her sanctuary. With infinitesimal movements, she lowered the trapdoor as she went. It still groaned from disuse, but it was a chance she had to take.

Once the door was completely shut, Hannah found herself clinging to the ladder in utter darkness. After a few moments her eyes adjusted and she could barely catch a glimpse of her surroundings from the faint moonlight streaming in through the tubes on the roof. Feeling her way, she descended until even that small light diminished.

She took another step down and suddenly found her left foot searching in vain for another rung. The ladder simply ended in the middle of nothing. With this new knowledge, she reformed her grip and crept back up until both of her feet were on rungs. Sliding one leg through the rungs, she straddled it and wrapped her left arm through the ladder. Taking a few minutes to calm her erratically beating heart, she listened for the unmistakable sounds of someone climbing the outer stairs.

In the distance she barely picked up the muted sound of a siren and prayed help was on the way. Knowing she couldn't take a chance on the police arriving before someone found her, she slid the pistol from her waistband. Staring up into the darkness, she waited.

Kane's trained eyes took in the scene within seconds of their arrival. A.L. had already been in contact with the local police department and they assured him help was on the way. As soon as Kane opened his door he could hear the echoing warble of a siren in the distance. He prayed they weren't already too late.

The relative silence was suddenly broken by several quick shots. The three agents crouched down into a defensive position behind the open car doors. Kane agreed wholeheartedly with the expletive Levi uttered as the last discharge rent the night.

Kane peered over the top of the car at the parking lot and the buildings beyond. Jason's car was parked at the front entrance and another sedan was situated a little to the right. Now that no weapons were being fired, footsteps and voices could be heard coming from the plant.

"Dreyer!" A.L. called from his awkward stance. Nothing. "Kane, call to Hannah."

Sucking in a breath, Kane was surprised to find he was actually able to make a sound. He waited a second and tried again. Only the occasional rumble of footsteps in the gravel-covered yard of the plant was his answer. Either Hannah wouldn't answer . . . or she couldn't. A bank of clouds floated across the moon eradicating its light. Kane took it as a sign. "I'm going in."

"Kane, wait," A.L. whispered, but it was too late. "Cover him."

"Don't tell me how to do my job," Levi growled from the other side of the car. "As soon as he makes it to the plant, I'm going. *You* cover *me*."

"Nothing like working with a bunch of damned hot-heads," A.L. said but nodded when Levi indicated his readiness.

A police car swung into the parking lot just as Levi rounded the side of the building and disappeared inside. A.L. quickly made his way to the officer and informed him of the situation. "I don't know what we've got inside yet."

"How many of your men are in there?" The officer unsnapped his holster indicating his desire to help.

"Three, I think," A.L. said, staring at the dilapidated structure. "And a woman. A civilian."

"Damn."

"My thoughts exactly." A.L. turned as three more cars wheeled in beside them. It took a few minutes to fill the new officers in on the situation. They couldn't risk making a move toward the building until they had a better idea of what was going on inside. "Grayson's got a radio with him, but we have to wait until he uses it. I can't risk contacting him. It might alert the enemy to his location."

"Right," one of the younger officers said. "You just let me know when you're ready to move."

A.L. moved back to his car and prayed the wait wouldn't be too long. He was used to action and he didn't relish playing the part of observer. He wanted to know what the hell was going on in there.

* * *

Kane hunkered down next to the front door, waiting for Levi to take his position. When he was fairly certain the other man was ready, he grabbed the door handle and shoved. "Now!"

In a split second he was through the door and rolling across the floor to avoid any bullets that might come his way. Out of the corner of his eye he saw Levi do the same thing on the opposite side of the room. Sliding behind a large oil drum, he took a minute to catch his breath and let his eyes adjust to the darkness. "Grayson."

"Yeah?" came the whispered reply.

"You see anything?"

"Hell, I've been in comas that weren't this black."

The two men listened for any sound that might indicate they weren't alone. After several minutes passed, Kane began inching his way toward Levi.

"What the hell?" He stopped as his foot struck something soft. A low moan came from the heap at Kane's feet and he dropped to his knees. For a split second he was afraid he had stumbled over Hannah, but the instant his hands touched the heavily muscled arm he knew it was a man. Digging into the front pocket of his jeans, he pulled out his lighter and allowed the flame to flicker long enough to identify Jason Dreyer. "Levi, get over here."

"What is it?" Levi asked, making his way across the room.

"Dreyer," Kane said with more emotion than he expected to feel. "He's down and it doesn't look good."

"Hannah," Jason barely managed to whisper as the two men began checking him for wounds. "Get her."

At the mention of Hannah's name, Kane forgot about

Jason's injuries and pulled the man closer. "Where is she?"

"Don't . . . know." His voice was soft, his words gurgled. "Hiding . . . so . . . damned . . . sorry."

"Dreyer," Kane called as he felt the man go limp against his arm. "Dreyer!"

"He's gone, man," Levi said as he removed Kane's hands from the man's jacket and lowered him to the cold concrete floor.

"Damn!"

"There's a little lady out there right now that probably wishes we'd get off our butts." Levi took a second to check the extra clips of ammunition in the pocket of his jacket before heading back out the side door. "You look in here. I'm going out into the yard. This is a hell of a place to play hide-'n'-seek."

Kane couldn't have agreed more. With only the pale glow of the moon lighting his path, he began to search every nook and cranny. His heart just about stopped when he came upon another body. This time the only remorse he felt was the fact he had not been the one to take the creep out. At least Jason had given as good as he got.

Despite the chill in the air, Kane could feel rivulets of sweat begin to trail down his chest and back. His jaws ached from grinding his teeth and holding back the screams welling up inside. *Where was she?*

In spite of every effort he had made, Hannah had managed to become a part of him. A part he had no intention of doing without. If he got her—no, *when* he got her out of this, he was going to take her back to that ramshackle farm she called home and tie her to the bedpost until she agreed to become Mrs. *Kane* McCord.

It came as a shock to him that he was even willing

to give up his career for her. Or at least the undercover part of it. He had done his duty in the field and was running dangerously close to burnout. It was time for the younger guys to take a stab at it. With Hannah in his life, he had a reason to come home in the evening. A purpose to live until the next day. *Come on, Hannah, let's get the hell out of here. I'm tired of this business.*

The snap of the front door opening caught his attention and he quickly reined in his scattered thoughts. There would be plenty of time for daydreaming once this was over. Sliding against the wall, Kane hurried back in the direction he had come. He could make out a man's shadow as it headed for the side door. Levi was out there. He might need backup. Catching the heavy metal door before it slammed shut, Kane silently slipped out after the man.

Okay, Kane, you can find me now. Hannah's muscles ached from her cramped position, but she was too terrified to move. There was no going down and she didn't dare go up. Long minutes had passed since the last gunshot had split the night, but she was too scared to ascend from her somewhat hellish haven.

Maybe she could go a little closer to the top. There was more light up there and she might be able to hear better. The wail of the siren was much closer now. Hopefully it would all be over soon.

With slow, careful movements, she slid the gun into place and began the climb. Her fingers were cramped from the fierce grip she maintained on the rungs and twice she had to scramble to hold on. *I should have taken Wanda Turnbow's aerobics class,* she thought as her breath became more labored.

The slick bottom of her loafers provided no traction

on the rungs and several times during her ascent, her foot slipped off the ladder. A faint sheen of sweat coated her brow and she wiped her face on the sleeve of her new sweater. She shuddered to think what the dirt and grease had done to the pale-pink top. *Don't be stupid, Hannah, it's only a sweater. This is your life we're dealing with here.*

With her hand-over-hand motion, she felt like the itsy bitsy spider climbing up the water spout. Hopefully the rain wouldn't come down and wash her out. Her strength was too sapped to make the climb again.

She was within a few yards of the trapdoor when the rung under her left foot broke. The sudden jerk on the ladder caused it to shift and the rungs popped out of the left side of the ladder. Her horrified scream echoed around her as the rest of the ladder broke loose and plummeted to the ground below.

"You're sure she's dead?" Sanchez asked.

"No one could survive a fall like that," came the muffled reply. Tony had barely been able to get away from the scene undetected. Lucero and Bennett hadn't been so lucky. He had just checked to make sure the agent was dead when the clattering of falling metal caught his attention. The woman's horrified scream had caused the hair on the back of his neck to rise. A dying woman's last cry for help wasn't something you forgot in a hurry.

"Did you actually see her?" Sanchez refused to believe what he was hearing.

"There was no way I could get close enough," Tony admitted. *"But I stuck around long enough to watch the ambulance. They weren't in any hurry."*

"Then she is dead." Sanchez knew that a slow am-

bulance only meant one thing—it was on the way to the morgue. "I am pleased."

"Thank you, sir." Tony hung up the phone and hefted the bottle of tequila by his bedside table. If Sanchez was happy, it would mean a bonus. After this mission, he could use one.

EIGHTEEN

The audience in the courtroom was varied. A few reporters were scattered along the back walls. One or two homeless people had managed to wend their way in out of the cold and past the guards. In the first seat on the left-hand side of the courtroom, directly behind the defendant, sat five large men. Each exuded a confident power that was missing from the elderly couple seated across the aisle.

Daniel and Betty McCord clung to each other as hopelessly desperate people tend to do. Hannah had been like their own daughter. And now she was gone. Without her testimony their son's killer would go free. It was the final insult.

"Your Honor, I wish to ask for a continuance of these proceedings." Brandon Emerson stood and presented his plea. There had been no word from anyone concerning the McCord woman and it was assumed she had perished in the fight. She had been his ace in the hole. His entire case hung on her testimony.

"What reasons do you present for such continuance?" The judge idly perused the papers in front of him.

Brandon spent the next five minutes listing every minute detail that might sway the judge in their favor. If he only had a few more weeks, they might be able to come up with some solid evidence that would convict the gloating scuzball at the other table.

Unfortunately, Judge Larson didn't see things his way and demanded the proceedings begin immediately.

For two days, Emerson and his associates tried to convince the jury that Roberto Sanchez was the worst kind of horror known to man. Much of what they had was circumstantial and the defense attorney bested them at every turn. Without Hannah, Sanchez would go free. The judge knew it, the jury knew it, and Sanchez knew it.

The defendant leaned back in his chair, a satisfied smile curving over his white teeth, as the prosecution prepared to wrap up their case. There was no way he would be found guilty. Not when his attorney had a list of eyewitnesses willing to swear he was attending a party the very same evening the poor officer had been shot.

"The witness may step down," the judge said to the parking valet who had testified to seeing a large black van speeding away from the vicinity of the restaurant. "Call your next witness."

Brandon Emerson opened his mouth to inform the judge his eyewitness was unavailable when the large double doors at the back of the courtroom suddenly swung open. Pivoting on the heel of his shiny leather loafer, Emerson watched as four large men strode through into the room.

The first man stood close to seven feet tall and could have played tackle on any pro football team in the nation. Even after he removed his black Stetson, he possessed an air about him reminiscent of Wyatt Earp or Marshall Dillon. A step behind him and to the right stood a smaller version. Still a large man, this one sported a white hat and a shiny badge pinned to the left side of his khaki shirt.

Emerson had to strain to catch a glimpse of the blond on the left side of the point man. In his perfectly tailored Armani suit and tie, he seemed out of place with the others. Especially, the last.

Although the other men commanded respect on sheer size alone, this man demanded it with his eyes. His hard, all-seeing gaze swept the courtroom before coming to rest on the couple seated in the front row. A flash of emotion glittered in those blue eyes. In a blink, it was gone.

"Gentlemen!" The judge banged his gavel to force the attention back to him. "What's the meaning of this?"

"Just makin' a delivery, Your Honor," said the first man. The men walked as a group past the startled spectators until they reached the witness stand. "You can go ahead, Mr. Emerson."

"But . . ." Brandon dared not give any credence to the brief thought flashing in his mind. Staring at the men in front of him, he shrugged. "Your Honor, I call Mrs. Hannah Elizabeth Hanson McCord."

Like the parting of the Red Sea, Levi, A.L., Eli, and Kane stepped aside to allow Hannah to climb the two steps. None of the men heard the cry of relief from the woman in the first row. Nor did they hear the bailiff swear Hannah in. All eyes were attuned to the bowed head of the defendant and the stunned army sitting behind him.

"Gentlemen, you may sit down."

Four pairs of very determined eyes glared at the judge. Four pairs of very muscular arms crossed over equally brawny chests. Four pairs of legs stood rooted to the spot.

"Or you may stand." Judge Larson nodded to the attorney. "You may continue, Mr. Emerson."

"Yes, sir!"

After three grueling hours of testimony, the judge called a recess and Hannah was allowed to step down from the stand. It wasn't over yet, but with her testimony, Sanchez stood a good chance of doing some serious jail time. Kane's arm automatically slid around her waist and she was grateful for his support. *For all their support.*

Hannah's Army. That's how she had begun to think of them over the last three days. They had lent her their strength and given her hope when hers was gone. They fussed over her, spoiled her, and waited on her hand and foot. It was every woman's fantasy.

Eli helped her forget with stories of their childhood. Levi made her laugh with his slow drawl and quick wit. A.L. catered to her need to nurture by eating everything she cooked. And Kane loved her. Willingly, and openly.

A small shudder rippled down her spine as she recalled just how close she had come to never knowing just how deeply their love ran. Her hands still sported several large cuts from grabbing onto the chain in the trapdoor just as the ladder fell from under her. She didn't know where her strength came from, but she managed to hold on until Levi pried the door open, Hannah still clinging to the chain.

Kane and A.L. stumbled around each other, trying to get to her once she was back on solid ground. They had almost shot each other in the dark, tense moments following Hannah's cry for help. She could still recall the horror on Kane's face when Levi told him how close she had come to winding up at the bottom of that cooling tower. And the relief when she fell into his arms and refused to budge, even when the ambulance arrived.

Levi and A.L. had taken care of the three dead men, handing them over to the attendants and assuring the local police their reports would be forthcoming. After what seemed like hours, Hannah found herself in a luxury suite at the best hotel with three bodyguards.

Her worries over Eli had been for nothing. She had bad-mouthed Kane for not having a contingency plan when he had already formulated one with Eli before they ever left Hanson. Kane, knowing there was no such thing as a foolproof plan, had arranged to meet Eli at his cabin in the mountains outside Ruidoso. Once the sheriff got the word that Kane and Hannah had disappeared, he took off without a word to anyone. Dolly was still upset by that maneuver.

For two days, Hannah and her army had stumbled over and around each other in the two-room cabin. The men had discussed the mistakes of the mission and she told them of Jason's confession. A.L. promised that Gloria Botello would see justice. They had played Monopoly, Scrabble and Jeopardy. Just when she had taken about all the pampering she could handle, it had been time to pack up and head for Albuquerque. Her only regret was not being able to be alone with Kane.

That, and the fact that she had been unable to see Roberto Sanchez's face when she stepped onto the witness stand.

"Kane!" Hannah's musings were interrupted as the McCords converged on their son. Tears sprang to her eyes as Kane swept his mother up in his arms and twirled her around. Kissing the petite woman soundly, he turned to his dad.

"I just don't understand," Betty McCord finally said when all the hugging and kissing was done. "They told us you were dead." Reaching to clasp Hannah to her side, she choked back another bout of happy tears. "Both of you."

"It's a long story, Mom," Kane said, wrapping Hannah in his arms. "And I could use a cup of coffee."

It didn't take Betty long to figure out that the woman she had welcomed as a wife for one son would soon be the mate of the other. There was only one more thing that would make her happiness complete. "And I could use a grandchild."

SHARE THE FUN . . .
SHARE YOUR NEW-FOUND TREASURE!!

You don't want to let your new books out of your sight?
That's okay. Your friends can get their own. Order below.

No. 44 DEADLY COINCIDENCE by Denise Richards
J.D.'s instincts tell him he's not wrong; Laurie's heart says trust him.

No. 119 A FAMILY AFFAIR by Denise Richards
Eric had never met a woman like Marla . . . but he loves a good chase.

No. 147 HANNAH'S HERO by Denise Richards
Kane was dead! Either Hannah was losing her mind or he *was* alive.

No. 100 GARDEN OF FANTASY by Karen Rose Smith
If Beth wasn't careful, she'd fall into the arms of her enemy, Nash.

No. 101 HEARTSONG by Judi Lind
From the beginning, Matt knew Lainie wasn't a run-of-the-mill guest.

No. 102 SWEPT AWAY by Cay David
Sam was insufferable . . . and the most irresistible man Charlotte ever met.

No. 103 FOR THE THRILL by Janis Reams Hudson
Maggie hates cowboys, *all* cowboys! Alex has his work cut out for him.

No. 104 SWEET HARVEST by Lisa Ann Verge
Amanda never mixes business with pleasure but Garrick has other ideas.

No. 105 SARA'S FAMILY by Ann Justice
Harrison always gets his own way . . . until he meets stubborn Sara.

No. 106 TRAVELIN' MAN by Lois Faye Dyer
Josh needs a temporary bride. The ruse is over, can he let her go?

No. 107 STOLEN KISSES by Sally Falcon
In Jessie's search for Mr. Right, Trevor was definitely a wrong turn!

No. 108 IN YOUR DREAMS by Lynn Bulock
Meg's dreams become reality when Alex reappears in her peaceful life.

No. 109 HONOR'S PROMISE by Sharon Sala
Once Honor gave her word to Trace, there would be no turning back.

No. 110 BEGINNINGS by Laura Phillips
Abby had her future completely mapped out—until Matt showed up.

No. 111 CALIFORNIA MAN by Carole Dean
Quinn had the Midas touch in business but Emily was another story.

No. 112 MAD HATTER by Georgia Helm
Sara returns home and is about to make a deal with the man called Devil!

No. 113 I'LL BE HOME by Judy Christenberry
It's the holidays and Lisa and Ryan exchange the greatest gift of all.

No. 114 IMPOSSIBLE MATCH by Becky Barker
As Tyler falls in love with Chantel, it gets harder to keep his secret.

No. 115 IRON AND LACE by Nadine Miller
Shayna was not about to give an inch where Joshua was concerned!

No. 116 IVORY LIES by Carol Cail
April makes Semi a very unusual proposition and it backfires on them.

No. 117 HOT COPY by Rachel Vincer
Surely Kate was over her teenage crush on superstar Myles Hunter!

No. 118 HOME FIRES by Dixie DuBois
Leara ran from Garreth once, but he vowed she wouldn't this time.

No. 120 HEART WAVES by Gloria Alvarez
Cass was intrigued by Peyton, one of the few who dared stand up to him.

No. 121 ONE TOUGH COOKIE by Carole Dean
Taylor Monroe was the type of man Willy had spent a lifetime avoiding.

----

voice an octave. Was Tezetta just being cautious or had